A Tale of Dogs & BONES

DEBBIE CHASE

This is a work of fiction. Names, characters, places, and incidents are products of the author's imagination or are used fictitiously and are not to be construed as real. Any resemblance to actual events, locations, organizations, or persons, living or dead, is entirely coincidental.

World Castle Publishing, LLC
Pensacola, Florida
Copyright © 2025 Debbie Chase
Hardback ISBN: 9798290075488
Paperback ISBN: 9798891264304
eBook ISBN: 9798891264311
First Edition World Castle Publishing, LLC, July 28, 2025
http://www.worldcastlepublishing.com

Cover: Cover Designs by Karen
Editor: Karen Fuller

CHAPTER ONE

June 1972 – Lambuck Woods

"Become a dog walker," they said, "It'll be fun," they said.

All those well-meaning people giving me advice, oh, helpful advice they thought, no doubt. After all, I was on a downer, a real Debbie Downer, as it's sometimes called. I'd been made redundant from my job as sales assistant in nearby Tedford's department store *"Stride and Sons,"* I'd lost Jason, my hot boyfriend, (and yet, thinking about it, was that really bad luck?), um, no, being as he was a bit of a fool, albeit, a good-looking fool, the good looks of course being what had turned my head.

Rock star looks had always appealed to me, and he'd certainly had that (well, rock star might be pushing it, how about local band looks?) You know what I mean, don't you? Long flowing hair, open neck shirt, a medallion lying on a smooth chest, skin-tight jeans, and t-shirts or sexy leather trousers. Yeah, I know, you're getting it, aren't you? How could I resist? He'd wanted the split, so yeah, my heart still hurt and, yeah, I know, it will get better.

Of course there'd been comments about my newly single state too, "Oh my God, you're over thirty, the clock's ticking, tick tock tick tock" but also more positive ones like, "You might meet somebody new," and "People will notice you, take a second glance when you're with a fluffy canine friend," and then with a knowing look, "Gives them an excuse to approach you and talk."

"What? I might meet somebody new whilst dog walking?" They'd all nodded, as they stared at me, their faces big frowns, as I said, "Oh yeah, great. Picture it, okay? I'm walking along, in slow motion maybe, you know, like in a film, my hair, tickled by a gentle breeze, streaming out behind me, just like a girl in a shampoo advert, a dog lead in one hand, oh, and the sun shining in a clear blue sky, no rain of course. After all, it never rains in a dream, does it?"

Excited by my story, they all nodded, "Yeah, yeah."

And then I went in for the kill, "And a bag of very aromatic doggy doo da dangling from my other hand. So, you really think that would make for a romantic encounter, do you?"

"Oh, give it a go, Mandy," I remember my friend Steph saying with a sigh, "Just give it a go," And then with a shrug, "It doesn't matter about the doggy bags, most men turn a blind eye to that anyway, and if he was a fellow doggy walker it would be no problem."

So, do you know what? I did! Yes, I gave it a try and landed a job almost immediately, walking a cute little Jack Russell named Bungle, a service dog for Becky, who lived nearby. "He needs a break from looking after me," she'd said, "A good long walk and plenty of treats, say, a couple of times a week?"

That one job opened the floodgates, and the business began to build up nicely, thank you very much. I even had some cute little cards made with my contact information in thick black letters, *"Mandy Morgan, Woof Woof Walkies, Dogwalker and Pet Sitter Extraordinaire."* Yeah, okay, I might be going a bit over the top by using the word "Extraordinaire," but you've got to bull yourself up a bit, haven't you? No? I disagree. If *I* don't, then I'm sure no one else will."

And something else, too, dog walking has helped me to perk up a bit. You know, being with animals, out in the fresh air, all that stuff has helped my mental health, so it's a win-win all round, eh?

So, I'm here now with my latest recruit, a rather chubby chocolate labrador named Max, who has, for some strange reason—another dog or a squirrel maybe?—darted into the bushes and became lost amongst the greenery, so that all I can see is a rather wide derriere (chocolate labs do tend to be on the chunky side), complete with a wildly wagging tail that slaps at the leaves, making them shiver and shake.

"Max, come out now!" I said in what I hoped was an authoritative way whilst fumbling desperately for his collar, his leash at the ready, sadly to no avail for whatever he was so intent on, there was no getting him away as he moved deeper and deeper into the greenery, sniffing and snuffling like a pig rooting out truffles.

"Let dogs sniff," they all said. But why, eh? I've heard they leave what might be known as a calling card, so was Max now sniffing out a new acquaintance? *Hi, I'm Ted, and I'm a Westie. I'm a 3-year-old rescue living with my humans, Monica and Stan, on Simonstone Way, Lambuck. We could meet if you like between the tea roses and the lilac…"* Whatever, he was still sniffing.

"Do you want a treat?" I asked hopefully, as the utterance of those words usually works like a charm, and he'd run to me, eyes bugging and tail going like crazy, but the manic tail wagging and snuffling into the depths of the dry summer earth continued. My heart thumping, I carried on pursuing him, pushing my way through the bushes, my hair getting caught up in the branches, nettles stinging my bare legs and hands.

"Max!"

Briefly he stopped but then the snuffling intensified followed by a couple of sharp yips that echoed through the air and then a short silence after which, all the bushes shaking, Max reappeared carrying something in his mouth, something round and white that, with aplomb, he dropped at my feet and then gazed at me with a smile, all his little white doggy teeth on display.

"Hmm," I said with a frown, "A present eh Max?" as I bent and picked up the object, staring at it curiously, not knowing at first what it was, and then with a shriek dropped it to the ground in horror where it rolled over and over and came to a stop face up so all its crooked teeth and deep eye holes were on display.

"A skull?" I screamed, putting my hands to my face, "Oh my God, Max, you've found a skull?" A wave of nausea came over me as I thought of the bony hand Jessica, the Border Collie, and I had found only a couple of days before. I'd hidden it away in a cupboard at home, thinking *"Out of sight, out of mind."*

Tongue lolling, Max's smile broadened, as if to say, "Yes, human, of course, and aren't I the clever one?"

Glad I was wearing gloves, I gingerly picked it up, holding it at arm's length, and inspected it with narrowed eyes. It was smooth, nothing sinister hanging from it, just empty white bone as if it had been licked by a pack of dogs or, chillingly, pecked clean by a murder of crows. It was so smooth and white and clean, apart from a tiny hole on the top and a thin black line running from it, that I wondered if it was real.

Maybe it was shop-bought and put here as a joke or a prank. I'd seen all manner of skulls in that groovy shop on Lambuck's High Street. *"The Tarot Cavern"* I think it's called and it sells weird and wonderful things like packs of glossy tarot cards and chubby Buddha's, and quirky things like black cat ornaments and skulls that weren't real but painted bright colors or covered in glitter, even a crow perched jauntily on the top of its cracked head.

Cautiously, I brought it closer and sniffed. Ugh, something primitive, earthy, wafted up my nose, belying the notion that it was from a shop, and, looking closer, I noticed tiny particles of dirt ingrained within the bone. With a shudder, I looked inside, peering in where the neck would have been, only to see something stuffed in there.

Curious, I rummaged with my fingers, eventually pulling out a piece of folded paper. It felt damp to the touch, as I smoothed it out and tried to read the typewritten words, the ink having faded a little, and the letter "E" at an odd angle and even more faded than the rest of it, *"So you've found the skull, hip, hip hooray, now maybe you'll look another day, and find a leg or perhaps an arm, maybe it's in the muck on a farm? Listen for the honk of a pig and be ready to get down and dig!"*

Frowning, totally mystified by this strange clue, my mind raced, imagining body parts strewn across all the local dog walking areas. Furtively, I glanced around, wondering if the skull and the clue were meant for me. Was somebody watching me right at this very moment? Somebody up to no good? A murderer, perhaps?

A shiver raced along my spine as, with a shudder, I

dropped the skull to the ground again and Max went straight to it sniffing avidly and then, turned his head, and gazed at me with his big brown eyes as if to say, "Come on human, what are you going to do?"

The bony hand came to my mind again, and the strange paper stuck on it saying simply, *"Now this is handy! Where's the other, I wonder?"* I pictured myself hiding it away at home with no thought whatsoever to tell the authorities, it was just a quirky find, and yet, now, having found a skull, a skull which just may belong to the hand, the thought, "I should take it to the police," ran through my mind. Bending down and grabbing hold of it yet again, I placed the offending item in my rucksack, amongst the doggy bags and the treats, and put the clue in my pocket. After which, I grabbed Max and firmly attached his leash, saying "Come on, boy," as I made my way home and then to the local constabulary with my two body parts.

***

March 1972 – Lambuck High Street and Lambuck Park – the day I met Michael Lawrence.

Okay, my name's Mandy Morgan, and I've always lived in Lambuck, a small town near the larger city of Tedford. I was born there and, well, I like it, I suppose, although perhaps I do because I haven't lived anywhere else, and I've nothing to compare it with. My mum and dad, the incomparable Angie and Stephen (Dad can't abide being called Steve), live nearby, as does my best friend, Stephanie, or Steph as she prefers to be called. I've no brothers and sisters, so Steph and her siblings are like family to me. I've got my own place, at long last (at the age of twenty-eight, yeah, I know I'm a slow one), and I'm loving it. It's just a small two-bedroom flat, but it's ace!

I was walking through Lambuck, my heart beating frantically as I headed to collect my first dog-walking job, a Jack Russell named Bungle. I think I mentioned him to you before? He was a service dog needing a break, according to his owner, Becky, who was confined to a wheelchair.

"He works all the time," I remembered her telling me, "He helps me by getting the washing out of the machine and putting it in the dryer, he brings me my medication and alerts me when I forget to take it as well as protecting me and the house from unwelcome visitors," She'd gazed at him fondly, just as he'd gazed at her, "I don't know what I'd do without my Bungle."

"Bungle's an unusual name," I'd said to her, "Where did you get it from?"

"Bungle?" she'd looked at me in surprise, "Why, the kid's programme on Telly, Rainbow. Surely, you've heard of Rainbow?"

I shook my head, feeling, by the expression on her face, that I'd made a number one faux pas and that I might even be banned from polite society for the foreseeable future.

"Yeah, Bungle the bear, Zippy, George, and Geoffrey, their human caretaker?"

I shook my head again as suddenly Becky began to sing, rooting me to the spot, my mouth open, "*Up above the streets and houses, rainbow climbing high, everyone can see it smiling over the sky. Paint the whole world with a rainbow...*"

"Ah yeah, I've heard that before," I said happily, suddenly remembering the tune from Steph's house and her little sister sitting on the floor, gazing with rapt adoration at the television screen, squeaky voices and raucous laughter floating around the room.

"Yes," she clapped her hands, "I knew you'd know it. Everybody does."

To my relief, Bungle jumped up, eager for his walk, as soon as I stepped inside the house. I'd imagined a reluctant dog hiding behind his owner, but at Becky's insistence, "Go fetch your leash, Bungle," off he trotted to retrieve the leash, which he laid with great reverence at my feet before looking up at me, his eyes shining and his expression hopeful.

A chilly wind was blowing, nipping at my cheeks until they turned a bright red, and my eyes were streaming with tears as Bungle and I briskly walked along Lambuck High Street. Above us, a blue sky and fluffy clouds floated, contrasting with the cold wind. However, I was snug in my waterproof dog-walking coat, wearing gloves and a hat, with a rucksack on my back filled with treats and doggy bags. Wow, what a way to make a living, right?

Bungle wore a smart quilted coat to protect his little furry body from the elements, yet I would imagine that the admiring glances from passersby and pats from all the little adoring kiddoes were more than enough to keep him warm. Confidently, he goose-stepped along, his head held high and a pleased expression saying, "Look at me, look at me," on his cute little face.

The park was busy with dogs running here, there, and everywhere, their walkers standing in huddles as if they were in a rugby scrum. The sweet smell of cut grass hung in the air, and a mower hummed in the distance. Children played on the swings and the slide, shouting excitedly to one another, their voices high and sweet.

Bungle showed his sinister side and began to bark

at all the larger dogs, stopping their friendly advances by emitting threatening growls from deep in his throat, giving them no choice but to slink back to their owners, bewildered expressions etched across their furry faces. Even a very large black fluffy ball of a dog backed off when Bungle emitted piercing shrieks and scary guttural growls in his general direction.

"Bungle, lighten up," I said, offering him a treat which he gobbled down greedily, whilst thinking about why Becky hadn't told me about these strange behaviors that he was showing.

"Hey, little dog syndrome, eh?" said a voice, as I looked up and saw a man walking towards me. A quite attractive man, wearing a blue waterproof coat and jeans, a woolly beany hat on his head, and a green doggy bag dangling from his hand that I knew without a doubt contained doggy doo da. Yet, despite that, he came close to me with a swagger and a smile with no embarrassment at all. Maybe I was the one who should lighten up. And yeah, little dog syndrome explained Bungle's behavior to a tee.

"Hi, Michael Lawrence," He held out a gloved hand which I tentatively shook, noticing that his grip was firm and tight, even though I'd only offered him the tips of my fingers. Well, I didn't know who he was, did I? He could be an axe murderer for all I knew! "Mick to my friends," he added with a grin.

"Nice to meet you," I said with a smile and, as I made to move on, my heart thumped hard, remembering what everybody had said about meeting somebody new whilst dog walking, he stopped me with the question, "Well, who are *you* then? I haven't seen you around here before." His blue gaze raked me quickly from the top of my head to the tips of my toes.

"Um, Mandy Morgan," I told him, "A new recruit to dog walking."

"Ah, yes, oh, you'll soon settle in. You've come at a good time. A fair number of us doggy walkers congregate here a few times a day. It's become more of a social thing, really," He gave a dry laugh before squatting down close to Bungle, "And who have we here then, eh?"

Straight away, Bungle edged back, soft growls coming from deep within his throat. Michael Lawrence laughed, "Yep, I'm right, eh? Little dog syndrome."

"This is my first time walking him," I said, "So maybe he's nervous? Or maybe I am?" I giggled inanely. Oh, if only I could stop such juvenile behavior.

A large white poodle looking cool in a bright blue harness suddenly appeared at his side, "Ah, this is my boy," said Michael Lawrence, "Meet Wilson."

"Wow, he's a gorgeous dog." I reached out a hand and stroked his soft fur. Wilson writhed in ecstasy at my touch and smiled prettily.

"He's a softy," said Michael Lawrence, "A poodle trait, I think."

"He's lovely," I replied and then, "Um, well, it's nice to meet you," as I made to move on again only to be stopped by an arm barring my way, a hand on my coat sleeve, "Hang on a minute, maybe we could have a chat, walk the dogs together. I could introduce you to the others." He motioned with his head at the huddle of dog walkers across the other side of the park.

I'm such a pushover, there's no doubt about it, as,

despite my initial reluctance, I allowed him to lead me across the park, where I shook hands and said hello so many times to Jack and Jo and Rachel and Lynne, oh and Uncle Tom Cobley and all, it would have been easier to have made a voice recording.

We made small talk after that, and Michael Lawrence asked me loads of questions about where I was born and how long I'd lived in Lambuck. And when I told him I'd lived here all my life, he had a bit of a bragging session telling me he was born and brought up in Lindon-on-Sea, an upmarket seaside town, which impressed me no end, but got just a bit boring after the tenth telling of the tale.

"It's the best place in the world," he said, "And we lived in a really big house, you know, like ten bedrooms and six bathrooms."

"It all sounds a bit too good to be true," I remembered thinking, as he harped on and on about Lindon-on-Sea so, after a couple more rounds of the park, and poor Wilson trying his best to make friends with Bungle who stoically ignored him, I said, "Thanks for that, but I must be making tracks. I must get Bungle back to his owner."

"Yeah," he gave me a blindingly white smile, "How about we go for a beer sometime, eh? Do you fancy that?" He paused for a moment and, when I didn't reply straight away, said, "Here, give me your number." With a grin, he pulled a pad from his pocket and held a pencil poised at the ready. I didn't want to give him my number, so I told him a little white lie. Of course, I have a phone at my place. After all, it was 1972!

"I haven't got a phone at my place yet," I told him.

He shrugged, "So, is there another way I can reach

you? What's your address?"

"Was this guy just a little too eager?" I pondered, eyeing him with suspicion. And what's he doing with a pad and pencil in his pocket? Always on the lookout for some gullible female to fall under his spell? I was not about to give him my address either. I gave him a narrow-eyed sort of weighing up smile, wondering if I should bother with him or not. But the thought of the look on Steph's face when I told her I'd clicked with an attractive man on my very first dog walk, doggy bag and all, won me over.

"I'll give you my mum and dad's number, okay?"

He nodded as I told him the number, saying each digit slowly and carefully, but just in the wrong order (I don't think that Mum and Dad would be over the moon if they started getting phone calls from strange men). He wrote it down and slipped the paper into his pocket.

"Thanks," He gave me a conspiratorial sort of smug nod, "I'll be in touch, yeah? Oh, and see you, Bungle."

Bungle snarled deep in his little throat and raised his trembling upper lip in an excellent Elvis Presley impersonation. I nodded and smiled as Bungle, seemingly happy to be leaving Michael Lawrence behind, trotted along at my side, the growl in his throat decreasing as we moved further and further away.

CHAPTER TWO

June 1972 – Trying to Crack the Clue

I've reread it to refresh my mind, *"So you've found the skull, hip, hip hooray, now maybe you'll look another day, and find a leg or perhaps an arm, maybe it's in the muck on a farm? Listen out for the honk of a pig and be prepared to get down and dig!"*

"Hmm, Applewood Farm," I thought, putting a finger to the map that was spread out in front of me in all its crinkled glory. "All I had to do was walk through the park and out onto Leeson Lane, follow it for around ten minutes, and, hey presto, it should lead out to the farm. Let's hope finding it is as simple as it sounds.

Applewood Farm wasn't the only farm in the area, but it was the nearest, so a good place to start, right? I was just about to collect Sophie the Chihuahua for a walk (yes, my business is building up very nicely, thank you), which was perfect timing, as the feeling that she would be able to help me crack the clue rested firmly in my gut.

Okay, before we set off, I've a confession to make. Please don't get mad, but I didn't go to the police after I found the skull. Yeah, you heard me right! I didn't go to the police with the hand and the skull. But, hey, I'm going to; it's just been postponed until I follow this clue, and if I find anything else, well, I'll go then. I mean, if I go with a hand, a skull, and maybe an arm, well, there's got to be something bad going on. That way, I could be assured the police would take me seriously.

Cars sped past us, honking manically if we didn't move out of the way quickly enough, and believe me, neither of us wanted to end up as roadkill. Like Clark Kent transforming into Superman, people change into monsters when they find themselves behind the wheel of a car.

After what seemed an eternity, the farmhouse came into view, and I puffed and panted as we went through the open gates and into a dusty-looking yard. Exhausted and hot, I took off my hat, gloves, and even my coat, and put everything into my rucksack. At the sound of the zip opening, Sophie, hoping for a treat, turned her head so quickly I was surprised she didn't get whiplash. I had a moment then, enjoying the sunshine as it warmed the top of my head, watching the little dog take treats from my fingers as delicately as she could.

I gazed around then, taking stock of my surroundings. The yard was empty, no tractors or wagons, no farmer, wearing a straw hat and saying, "ooh ah, ooh ah," whilst flitting from barn to barn. It's quiet too, with no honking of geese, bleating of sheep, or mooing of cows; in fact, no sound at all. Just an air of dejection like a puppy with its tail between its legs. Hey, just like Sophie, who stands gazing around, also taking it all in, her face a little question mark as if to say, "Where am I? A dirty farmyard? Some walk this is!"

I noticed the farmhouse windows were boarded up with thin sheets of plywood, and there was a padlock on the massive front door, yet I was able to peer through its dirty glass pane into the hallway, where I could see a mass of unopened letters and flyers scattered all over the floor. Hmm, whoever left the clue had no idea that the farm was closed, as the clue indicated a place where a lot of action was going on, with the honking of pigs and all that.

Disappointed, we walked past the farmhouse to the barns, my footsteps and Sophie's paw steps treading through dust and dirt, piles of dirty straw and, by the smell of it, cow and horse dung. Oh my, the odor was foul and seemed to get worse and worse the nearer we got to the barns. Even Sophie stopped in her tracks and scrunched up her nose. Suddenly, as if in a blinding flash of light, the words "pig" and "dig" came into my mind. Hadn't the clue used those very words?

"Come on, Sophie," I said, as she gazed at me quizzically, "We need to find the pigsty."

My footsteps crunched as we passed the farmhouse and the barns, where, in the distance, I could see a higgledy-piggledy wall and, in the far distance, fields and trees baking beneath the hot sun. There was the smell of dry earth and the soft humming of bees, and then a more pungent stench of muck as the pigsty came into view. Sophie edged forward, pulling hard on her leash, squeaking like a little mouse, excited and aware that there was work to be done.

As soon as I let her off her leash, she shot into the muck of the pigsty, yipping and yapping like crazy. I followed her, armed with a garden trowel that I'd so cleverly brought with me and holding my nose, desperately trying to ignore the awful, sunbaked stench, we both began to dig.

***

April 1972

As I knew it would be, Steph's face was a mixture of confusion and downright jealousy when I told her about my meeting with Michael Lawrence. She didn't even believe me at first.

"I don't believe you, Mandy Morgan," she said, "It's

just not possible that you've met some gorgeous bloke on your very first dog walking job." She giggled inanely, "Not after everything we said. All the teasing and that. You're making it all up."

"I'm not making it up," I said, "But he's not gorgeous, he's quite attractive, but, well…"

"Well, what?"

"I'm not sure, there's something about him…he's just a bit well,"

"Well, what?"

"A bit too keen?"

"No bloke can be too keen, Mandy. You need your head seeing to, you do. I'd grab him with both hands if I were you."

"Yeah, but you're not me, are you?"

"Oh, you mean you're on the rebound, you know, from Jason?"

"No, well, I don't think so. I'm just not sure if he's my type."

"Is it because of the doggy bag?"

"Steph, I'm not that shallow! And it didn't bother him; he seemed not to care that he was carrying a bag of doggy doo da. He was very cool, calm, and collected. Anyway, it goes with the territory, the job."

"Wow, what a guy," she replied as if in awe.

It was true, though, every word I said to Steph was true. I wasn't sure about him. Something about his presence made me feel tingly all over. Oh, not in an excited way, but more in a scary way, and I don't know why. I've only seen him a couple of times, but the feeling has been the same both times. He's a bit weird, volatile, and so changeable that I'd bet a pound that I don't change my underwear as often as he changes his personality.

And as well as that, the dogs I walk don't like him, and do you know what? I trust the dogs. I trust their instincts. Wilson was the only dog who didn't seem to have an aversion to him. I'm meeting him tonight, in the local pub, The Rabbit & Bear in Lambuck (the man that is, not the dog), and I'm fully intending to break it off. And yet, what is there to break off anyway, a couple of beers and a Babycham? Oh, and I'll do it if I can find the courage.

***

April 1972 – The Rabbit and Bear Public House

"I met her in a pub down in old Soho, where they drink champagne and it tastes just like cherry cola, c-o-l-a cola…"

I saw Michael Lawrence before he saw me (or Mick as he'd asked me to call him). He sat, slumped forward, his forearms on the table, a pint of beer in front of him. He held a cigarette between two fingers, a little orange glow, the smoke curling lazily in the air. He was wearing his usual blue jeans and a blue shirt, a black overcoat over the top instead of his waterproof walking jacket. Maybe his idea of getting dressed up? At least I'd tried and was wearing my favorite flared jeans and a black flowered gypsy top. I'd even put on a touch of blue eyeshadow and a slick of lip gloss. *"She walked up to me and asked me to dance. I asked her her name, and in a dark brown voice, she said, Lola, L-o-l-a, Lola, la-la-la-la Lola…"*

Jack, the landlord, gave me a nod as I walked in and said, "Your man has put a Babycham behind the bar for you, shall I bring it over?"

"Oh, yes, please, Jack," I said, not sure about the words

"your man," but I let it go. Mick looked up and saw me, as I strolled over and said, "Thank you for the drink," and sat down opposite him.

He nodded, "Alright then?" He stubbed his cigarette out on a large ashtray, "Whitbread Trophy Bitter," imprinted around its sides in large black letters. I noticed, as if for the first time, that some of his fingers were stained yellow, making my stomach churn.

Jack came over with the Babycham, already poured from the small bottle into a proper Babycham glass, decorated with the trademark prancing fawn and the word "Babycham" in block capitals around the base. "There you go, love."

"Thank you, Jack."

I raised my glass to Mick and said, "Cheers," but before I could clink glasses, he sat back, his face long and disapproving, his arms crossed over his chest.

"Well, that's the way that I want it to stay, and I always want it to be that way for my Lola, La-la-la-la Lola..."

"Anything the matter?" I asked, as I took a sip of the Babycham, feeling the bubbles pop up my nose, making me laugh.

"What do you think you're laughing at?"

Taken aback by his tone of voice, I said, "Nothing," and then shrugged, "Well, actually the Babycham bubbles." I giggled again, yet the downcast look stayed on his face, "Did you get out of bed the wrong side this morning or something?" I may have looked calm on the outside, but my heart was racing fast on the inside, so I had to take a deep breath to calm myself.

"You know Jason Rogan, don't you? You went out with him, didn't you?"

"Well, I'm not the world's most masculine man, but I know what I am and I'm glad I'm a man, and so is Lola…"

"Yes, I did. A few months ago, now, but we had an amicable split," frowning, I said, "Is that what's put you in a bad mood?"

Ignoring my question, he tittered a little (yes, tittered!) and said, "Amicable? I heard he dumped you for someone else."

I shrugged, the hurt I'd felt at the time coming back to haunt me, "Perhaps," I replied, "But it was a few months ago now. All in the past."

"You used to come here with him, didn't you?"

He sipped his beer and then wiped his upper lip where foam from the creamy head had clung. I felt a sudden revulsion towards him, but nodded, as memories came back. I gazed around the familiar interior of the pub, with its thick black beams on the walls and ceiling and massive old fireplace, a sluggish fire burning to ward off the chill of the April evening.

A couple was sitting at the table next to us, holding hands and gazing into each other's eyes. A group of men stood at the bar, laughing and joking, whilst a couple of little old men played a game of dominoes, the dominoes clicking faster and faster against the table as their excitement mounted.

With a sudden spurt of anger, I said, "Yes, I did, but that's hardly any business of yours." With a sudden resolve, I drained the Babycham and put the empty glass carefully on a beer mat. "Look, Mick, I have to go now and, um, perhaps it's better we don't meet socially anymore, we…"

"Why?" he cut in, "Why, Mandy? What's your problem?"

"Oh, no problem," I said airily, not wanting to upset him. I didn't trust him not to vent his anger, "I'm just really busy at the moment and, um…"

"Huh, you haven't even got a valid excuse, have you?" He sat back in his chair again, arms folded across his chest like a sulky child, which was precisely what he was, a big, sulky manchild. Jealous, it seemed, about a previous boyfriend, confirming to me for definite that he wasn't somebody I wanted to see regularly.

"No," I thought to myself, "No valid excuse, just a gut feeling," but said out loud, "We can still walk our dogs together."

"Oh really," he said sarcastically. "I knew you weren't for me, anyway. I mean, fancy not even getting dressed up for a date. Jeans and a flowery top? I mean, how many women keep on their tatty old jeans, eh?"

He drained his pint and stood up and, using the table for support, leaned forward close to my face, "You didn't even give me a proper phone number, did you?" I blanched at that.

"You'll regret this, Mandy Morgan, you really will." He walked out then, the door swinging shut behind him.

I breathed a sigh of relief and sagged into myself like a burst balloon, just for a split second, hurt at what he'd said about my clothes. They weren't tatty by any means. I was tempted to go to the bar and order another Babycham, but on second thought, I decided to go straight home.

I felt weird and strange and needed the solace of my little kitty cat, Herman. Thank God I had him waiting for me, keeping at bay the dreaded, stupid, lonely thoughts that seemed to plague me nowadays. I picked up my bag and stood up to leave, when a voice stopped me, "Hi, um, are you okay?"

As I turned around, I came face to face with a man of such sheer gorgeousness that I almost sat down again in shock. He was tall with a mop of blonde hair that fell in a sweep over his forehead, and green eyes surrounded by thick black lashes. It was a pet peeve of mine that some men were lucky enough to have such lovely eyelashes, and all without the aid of mascara. I spent ages in front of the mirror trying to get mine to look like that.

"Um, no, I'm fine, thanks. I was just about to leave." My heart thumped uncontrollably, so I had to take a deep breath, but it continued to thump, like someone banging on a drum.

"Yeah, so am I," he began, as he shrugged on his jacket, a black leather biker-type jacket at that, which made my heartbeat even harder, "I'll accompany you if you like. I don't like the look of the fella you were with. Do you live far from here?"

"No, about a ten-minute walk, but I'm okay, there's no need." I shook my head, noticing his assessing, narrow-eyed gaze, prompting me to say, "No, really, I'm okay." I saw the group of men at the bar, of which I assumed he was one, gazing at us with interest; their raucous conversation had fallen silent for the moment.

"So, he's no threat to you then?" He looked at me intently, late sunlight shining through the window, lighting the mossy green of his eyes.

"Well, okay, he does make me feel a little uncomfortable." I had a split second of worry that Mick would be waiting outside and be angry if he saw me with this gorgeous man.

"Yeah, I'm not surprised. He was well out of order." He gazed at me and his eyes swept over my body, seeming to take in every inch, "There's absolutely nothing wrong with the way you're dressed." A lovely warm feeling slowly crept through my body as he carried on speaking, "In fact, you look great."

John Kongos started to sing from the jukebox, *"Make your bed up high, pray into the sky, close the window, close the door, makes no difference if you're rich or poor..."* The music faded a little as we stepped outside, *"Get on your knees, scream please, that man just loves to tease. Try to run, get a gun..."* He held out a hand, and said, "Jay Sutherland at your service."

"Mandy Morgan," I replied, as we clasped hands. His hand was very warm, enveloping mine as if he were a big cat and I a tiny kitten, sending shivers racing along every knobbly vertebra of my spine. I gazed around, afraid that Mick would be lurking in a dark corner, waiting to spring out at me, but there was nobody there, and I breathed a sigh of relief.

My companion smiled cheekily, creating cute dimples in both cheeks, and said, "Pleased to meet you."

"Likewise," I said, feeling stupid as a severe case of tongue-tiedness (is that even a word?) came over me as we strolled along, me trying to make polite conversation, whilst thoughts of "Why is this man helping me?" raced through my mind. Jay Sutherland chatted easily, helping me to open up and tell him about the dog walking and how I'd met Michael Lawrence. "I told him we shouldn't meet socially anymore, and he didn't take it too well," I said.

He nodded thoughtfully as I said, "Anyway, this is me." I nodded towards the building where I had a ground-floor flat. "Thank you for walking me home."

"It was a pleasure," he replied, "But look, if you have any problems, give me a ring." Fumbling in his jacket pocket, he found a tatty piece of paper and scribbled down his number, "There's something about that guy I didn't like. Okay?"

My face burned a deep red as I took the paper from him. With a cheeky wink, he said, "Take care," and walked away. I watched him go, my heart still thumping hard, wondering if I'd ever see him again.

"Probably not," I thought with a sigh, and there was no way I'd ring him. "Men that look like Greek Gods just aren't for Mandy Morgan, I'm afraid."

I unlocked the door and went into the hallway. Herman rushed out to greet me with excited meows. I picked him up and nestled my face into his fur, feeling glad that he was here, while thoughts of Michael Lawrence raced through my head. I felt nervous about how he would be the next time I saw him dog-walking. Maybe I should take Bungle with me, or Sophie, small as they are, they'd make mincemeat out of him if he turned on me in any way.

In the sitting room, I noticed I still had the slip of paper the gorgeous Jay Sutherland had given me screwed up in my hand, so I smoothed it out and stared at for a long time, before folding it carefully and putting it into my bag. Darkness stood hard at the window, so I took a quick peek outside to reassure myself that no one was lurking about. I pulled the curtains across, feeling safe now and far away from the prying eyes of Michael Lawrence.

CHAPTER THREE

June 1972 – Lambuck Police Station

"Okay, love," said the desk Sergeant, who looked on the verge of erupting into a great belly laugh, "So you're saying that all three of these packages contain a part of a human body?"

"Yes," I nodded, "There's a hand, look, this small one. A skull here in the skull-shaped one," I gave a little giggle, "And this long one is the top part of an arm. The humerus, I think it's called."

"Oh, thanks for that." Smirking, he nodded his head and then said, "You're not having me on, are you?"

"No, certainly not."

The sergeant, his lanyard stating his name, Sergeant Tony Crawford, gazed at me suspiciously as he unwrapped each piece and put them on the desk between us.

"You see," I said, "I wasn't having you on."

"No, I can see that." He looked taken aback now, the smirk and the laughter completely gone from his craggy face.

Luckily, I'd chosen a good time to bring them to the Police Station, as it was quiet and nobody was sitting on the hard chairs in the reception, and no phones were ringing, creating a disturbance. I had the full attention of the Sergeant, which was great as I wanted to get this over and done with, so I could go home and live my life as happily as I had before the body parts had turned up to plague my every waking moment with worry and doubt.

"I don't even know if they're real," I told him, "They could be plastic body parts. I've had them for a couple of months now, and there's no smell from them or," I shrugged, "You know, anything like that."

The sergeant raised his voice an octave, "You've had them for a couple of months? Why? Why didn't you bring them in before?"

"Well," I faltered a little, my heart beating hard and fast at the Sergeant's nasty glare and tone of voice, "It wasn't until my little dog Sophie found the arm that I thought it could be something serious." My mind went back over the day we'd found it, the fear and revulsion I'd felt as it was revealed beneath the muck in the pigsty and Sophie's excited yips echoing around the deserted farmyard.

"Oh, so not even finding the skull alerted you to possible foul play then?" He brandished the skull close to my face, the empty eye sockets seeming to stare into mine, and for the first time, I wondered who this person had been, this person who had had a life cut short, a life with periods of worry and happiness just as I had. That maybe had enjoyed a drink of Babycham or a pint of beer, had loved sweet things but hated liver and onions, or enjoyed Top of the Pops but not the ten o'clock news.

I swallowed hard, my face on fire as the Sergeant said, "I'm going to have to get our Detective Inspector to look at these and to have a quiet word with you. Please, take a seat, Miss er, Mrs."

"Miss," I said, "Mandy Morgan. Look, Sergeant, do you think there may be other body parts buried in the local area? Maybe I should keep looking, eh? There might be a whole body, what do you think?"

"A hand, a skull, and the top part of an arm or the humerus do not a full body make," intoned the sergeant,

"What? That doesn't make sense!"

"No, neither do you. You make no sense at all!" He leaned forward close to me, his elbows on the desk between us, "In the way that I find it a bit strange that somebody would keep body parts in their own home for such a length of time without reporting it to the police!"

I opened my mouth to speak, but the Sergeant carried on relentlessly, "So, in your daily endeavors, if you do find anything else, you bring it here straight away, never mind stashing it away for two or three months, okay? In the meantime, sit yourself down and wait, right?"

I nodded and then said, "Oh, and there are these as well." I put the clues down in front of him, "The clues that came with each body part..."

Perplexed, the Sergeant scratched his head, "Clues?"

"Yes, well, the first one, the one that came with the hand, isn't a clue, but the other two are."

I turned to walk away when the Sergeant said, "Hang on a minute, you didn't mention any clues before." He read each piece of paper, his eyes scanning the words, the clue that came with the arm still fresh in my mind, "*So you've got the arm, well, aren't you good, I really didn't think you would. If you enjoy a drink, look behind a keg, you never know, you might find a leg!*" Whilst reading it, I'd noticed the same thing as the other clue, the "E" at an odd angle, the faded type, indicating it was the same typewriter as before, and perhaps the same person.

"Hmm, I think you should sit down in the reception, Miss Morgan. I've a phone call to make."

Obediently, I sat down, even more glad now that the

reception was quiet. I certainly didn't want anybody else to know about this. I didn't want anybody, bat ears flapping, to be sitting here right now, listening in. I hadn't told anybody about the body parts at all, not Mum and Dad, not even Steph, and certainly not Michael Lawrence. Oh no, not even when I'd had a Babycham or two. And I wouldn't ever, and that's the truth. The Sergeant interrupted my thoughts, "Miss Morgan?"

"Yes?"

"Our Detective Inspector will be down in a bit. He wants a word with you, so you stay where you are. Right?"

A dart of apprehension overcame me, and I wondered with a heavy heart whether I was in trouble for not reporting this sooner and what the Detective Inspector would do with me. Did this sort of behavior warrant a prison sentence?

Nodding sadly, I said, "Yes, okay. I'm not going anywhere."

The Sergeant slowly shook his head, saying brusquely, "Too right you're not."

The phone suddenly rang, sounding loud in the quiet room, and the sergeant answered. "Good morning, Lambuck Police Station," just as the door opened, and a man, looking very much the worse for wear and smelling strongly of alcohol, staggered in and made a beeline for me, which was hardly surprising as I was the only person there, apart from the Sergeant of course, but he was sitting behind a desk, safe and protected.

"Hiya love, got a penny to spare for a poor old hungry man?"

"No, sorry," I said, "I don't carry money as a rule. Well, not pennies anyway."

"Oh, the Queen, are you?"

I shook my head as the Sergeant's voice rang out across the room, "Out, Edgar, right now." I noticed he still clutched the telephone receiver, his hand firmly over the top of it.

"Oh, come on, Sarge."

"Out, or I'll arrest you."

"Arrest me then. At least I'll get a sandwich and a cuppa, oh, and a warm place to sleep tonight."

"Out!"

"Yeah, do as you're told, Edgar mate," said a different voice, and I turned around to see a familiar face, his blonde floppy hair and green eyes as captivating as the first time I'd seen them. He smiled, and those dimples appeared in his cheeks like magic. Oh my, he definitely was a Greek God.

Catching my eye, he said, "Excuse me for a moment," as he opened the door wide and said to the drunk, "Go on, out you go, Edgar."

"All I want is something to eat. Take pity, eh? Me stomach's grumbling like a bloke who's just lost on the horses."

With a rueful shake of the head, the Greek God said, "Here," and I saw him push a five-pound note into the drunk's hand, "Make sure you get something to eat, Edgar, and not more to drink."

"Thanks, Sir," he replied, as he staggered out of the door, "You've got a kinder heart than him!" He pointed to the sergeant, who was still talking on the phone, and the sergeant retaliated by making a silly face as the door closed behind him.

"Sorry about that, um, Miss Morgan?"

"That was kind of you."

He shrugged, "It's nothing. He comes in here all the time. Poor bloke. You're Mandy Morgan?"

"Yes. Do you remember me? The Rabbit and Bear?"

The Greek God nodded his head sagely, "I did wonder if it was the same Mandy Morgan. And then I thought, well, it must be. After all, there couldn't possibly be two of you, could there?"

"Wow, I had no idea you were a policeman," And then with a sudden sinking of my heart, "So that's why you helped me that night, is it?"

"No, not at all. I was off duty when I saw you in the pub, so I didn't have to help if I didn't want to." He gave a mock bow, "Detective Inspector Jay Sutherland at your service." His hand enveloped mine again, so warm and reassuring, and his lovely mouth turned up in a smile. Oh my, I was in Heaven until he brought me quickly back down to earth with the words, "Now, I need to have a serious word with you." He indicated with his head, "Follow me."

Standing up, my heart beating hard, I followed the attractive figure of Detective Inspector Jay Sutherland from the reception area, wondering what on earth was going to happen to me now.

***

"Body parts?" Steph exclaimed, almost choking on her cheese sandwich.

"Shh," I said quickly, hastily peering over my shoulder, hoping that no one was listening in on our conversation. After all, there were a lot of people about, especially here in Woolworths Café, a notoriously busy place at any time of day, and as it was lunch time, all the world and her wife were in here grabbing a quick bite before going back to work.

Her raised tone alerted the two women at the next table who, reeking of well-to-do-ness, (if that's a word?") and fully togged out in designer clothes, as well as flesh-colored stockings and short black leather gloves, thick red lipstick smeared on their lips, glanced curiously, probably wanting to know more about the "body parts."

Steph was on her lunch break from her job in Lambuck's only building society, "The Providential," and I'm in between dogs, Bungle the service dog and Sophie the mean Chihuahua, to be precise.

"Shh," I said, "This goes no further, Steph, okay?"

She shook her head, tiny little shakes, and her big brown eyes were wide over the top of her sandwich, as if she was watching a horror film behind the safe confines of a cushion.

"I've told the police." I took a bite of my sandwich, the tangy flavors of cheddar cheese and Branston pickle exploding in my mouth.

"Police?" She leaned forward in her chair and, after eating the last of the sandwich, even dabbing at the crumbs on her plate as if she were starving, picked up her cup and took a deep draft of aromatic coffee.

"Yes, of course, although I got a right roasting for not taking them in sooner. Apparently, I was withholding evidence."

"Really?"

"Yeah, that's what he said. I didn't know that, though, did I?"

"Who's he?" She shrugged, "Who said that?"

Leaning closer to her, I said, "The gorgeous Detective Inspector Jay Sutherland."

"Wow!"

"Yeah, he looks like a Greek God."

"A Greek God?"

The two women turned around again at the words, "Greek God," so, with much scraping on the tiled floor, we turned our chairs just a little and gave them a clear view of nothing but our backs. I meant it when I said this conversation could go no further.

"Good one, Mandy," said Steph, "Now tell me more about this Greek God."

My mind went back to the interview with Detective Inspector Jay Sutherland in the small room where I was alone with him, with its one high window and cold radiator. We'd sat opposite each other on uncomfortable, hard chairs, the three body parts lined up in a row on the table in between us.

"So, why didn't you bring these items," He indicated towards them with his head, "to the police before now?"

I was silent, my cheeks burning and my head hanging, partly because I was ashamed and had an unattractive red face, and partly because I didn't want to look up and see the disgust in the Detective Inspector's lovely eyes. Admiration, yes, but disgust? No!

"It's no good being silent, Miss Morgan, fess up, come on."

"It's Mandy, please call me Mandy. I'm sorry, it's just that," I looked up then and caught his green-eyed gaze, "I didn't think anyone would believe me, and that you might think I'd committed a crime."

He gave a great sigh, "What? That we might think you're a murderer and you've cut up your victim and brought the body parts in to show us?"

I giggled, "Well, yes, you could think that, but…"

"And could it be true?"

"No, of course not. I found these body parts," I pointed to them with a shaky finger, "With a little help from my dogs. I'm a dog walker, you see."

"Ah, I see."

"I found the hand first, although there was no clue on it, except for something about it being handy. It was a total shock finding the skull, well, one of my dogs, Max, he found the skull, and that did have a clue which I wanted to crack before I came here."

"So, then you found the arm with the clue?"

I nodded.

"And the man you were with, in the pub, do you think this has anything to do with him?"

Frowning, I said, "Why do you ask that?" A little frisson of something like shock ran through me.

He shrugged, "I'm not sure. You seemed a little afraid of him when I saw you in the pub that night. I'd been watching you both, you see."

"Well, he's a fellow dog walker. When you saw us, that was only the second time I'd been for a drink with him. I didn't want to go, but he insisted. I suppose he could be controlling."

"So, you finished the relationship that night?"

"Yes, I did, although it wasn't a relationship as such, but, well, he got angry. That's why he stormed out."

"Yeah, I got that." He was quiet for a moment or two, his eyes narrowed, making my heart beat faster and faster, "Well, whether you knew it or not, you have been withholding evidence. The body parts could be part of a missing person's remains, for example, a cold case that may be solved with new evidence. You should have brought them in immediately." His lovely green eyes flashed as he spoke, the anger he felt towards me evident on his face.

"I'm sorry."

"Yes," he said, his expression softening, "I know you are."

"So, you're not going to arrest me?"

He laughed a little, and a smile lit up his face, deepening his dimples. Taking advantage of his good nature, albeit temporary, I leaned forward, my forearms on the table, "I know we can find the next bit, a leg by the sound of it, from the latest clue. It's easy."

"Oh no," He slowly shook his head, "You won't be looking for any more body parts or clues, Mandy…"

"Why?" I wailed. Yes, despite myself, I showed myself up and wailed in front of the gorgeous Detective Inspector Jay Sutherland.

He looked at me sympathetically, "The case is in the hands of the police now."

"But my dogs, they can help. I can help. Please let me."

"Look, Mandy, I'm not going to arrest you now for what you've done, but if you carry on with it, then I will have to, okay?" I remembered he'd leaned in towards me, his face very close to mine, "I'd have no choice."

"Mandy? Mandy?" A voice cut into my thoughts, bringing me back to the present where Steph's worried face loomed in front of me, "You really should be careful, you know, I don't think I could bear to visit you in prison," Grimacing, she shook her head, "It's not my scene at all," She looked at her wrist, "I've got to get back to work. I'll get killed for being late."

"Oh, don't worry, Steph, I won't be going to prison, oh, and you won't get killed for being late."

"Huh, want to bet?"

She stood up, seeming to tower over me, elevated as she was on her six-inch platform shoes. "Hey, what happened to that dog walking bloke you were going to meet up with?"

"Oh, long story," I said, "And old news. We need a full night out for that."

She giggled, "Okay, I'll be in touch then."

I watched her walk away, a striking-looking woman, her thick brown hair trailing down her back, her coat pulled in tight at the waist, and the platform shoes making her look tall and willowy, even though she was only five feet five inches, the same height as me.

"Dogs," I thought to myself as I walked towards the door, checking my rucksack for doggy bags and treats, I began to psych myself up for a walk with Sophie the mean Chihuahua, all the while thoughts of Jay Sutherland went through my mind, making my heart race, and what a turn up for the books that he was with the police.

I thought of the latest clue as well, even making up my mind that I'd have a crack at it. After all, what did it matter if I was arrested? As Edgar the drunk said, you could get a hot drink, a sandwich, and somewhere to put your head down for the night, and, also, if Detective Inspector Jay Sutherland was involved, it could only be a good thing, right? I wouldn't mind spending time alone with him in a cell.

CHAPTER FOUR

June 1972 – Cracking the Latest Clue

"A keg," I thought, "A keg of beer? A keg of beer is often associated with a pub, as is the phrase 'enjoy a drink.' So, the keg could be in a pub or outside a pub. The *Rabbit and Bear*, maybe? A keg from *the Rabbit and Bear*? Close to home, so first port of call.

I looked at the clue again, to keep it fresh in my mind, *"So you've got the arm, well, aren't you good, I really didn't think you would. If you enjoy a drink, then look behind a keg, you never know, you might find a leg!"*

My new dog, Bella the Labrador, whined impatiently, her face a mask of despair, eager to be on her walk. Although with her front legs crossed, I had a pretty good idea why she was in such a tearing hurry.

"Come on, Bella," I said, "A quick trip to the *Rabbit and Bear* before we hit the park."

The pub looked summery, the exterior hung with colorful, sweet-smelling hanging baskets, and the door stood wide open, letting in tendrils of warm summer sunshine. A blackboard was propped up outside advertising its food choices. Enticing people in with such delights as chicken and chips in a basket, a ploughman's, scotch eggs, and fish and chips. My tummy rumbled at the thought of all that lovely food, but no, I had more pressing things to attend to today, and eating wasn't one of them… yet.

The board advertised real ale, which was becoming popular, with my dad being one of its biggest fans. No wonder one of the ales on offer sounded familiar. At 8% (wow, could Dad really drink strong beer like that without falling over?), the ale, *Love is Noise,* was *"big, fruity and with a great body."* No wonder the *Rabbit and Bear* was so popular.

But I digress, the front of the pub wasn't something I was interested in now, even though I do enjoy a Babycham or two, but the back of it is. The reason being that I knew that the beer was delivered to the back in a big wagon. I'd seen Jack the landlord opening the doors to the cellar, allowing a couple of big, muscly men to manhandle the beer kegs down into its sour-smelling depths, no doubt receiving a couple of pints afterwards, for all their hard work. Large silver beer kegs were always piled haphazardly against the pub's brick wall, some as high as two or four, and others towering like a block of flats, at eight.

Off her leash, Bella immediately started to sniff around the kegs, pushing her nose into the cracks in between them, sniffing, her nose twitching, and her body wiggling as if she was excited. At the same time, her tail thrashed about, almost knocking down an adjacent pile of kegs. I imagined them crashing to the ground and rolling along Lambuck High Street, people staring in disbelief.

I was standing, rooted to the spot, as Bella began to make low, moaning sounds from deep in her throat. And then, to cap it all, there was the familiar sound of an engine and a wagon, Watneys Ales emblazoned along its side, coming lumbering around the corner.

"Oh no, surely it's not delivery day," I thought, and then, "Bella, come on, we have to go," but would she listen to me, no! A big fat no! She carried on with the sniffing and tail wagging, then growled just as the wagon stopped and idled at the kerb, engine throbbing, and the faint sound of T-Rex music drifted out from the radio, *"Metal guru, is it you? Yeah, yeah, yeah..."* Quickly, I clipped on her leash and tugged at it, and said, "Come on, Bella," but stubbornly she refused to move, digging her paws into the ground, carrying on with the whining and moaning. Why had she decided to be naughty in a time of such crisis?

The wagon's engine cut off, and all was quiet and still when Bella growled again and suddenly lunged at something, making the kegs wobble dangerously, and then grabbed whatever it was in her mouth, just as the wagon doors opened and two men got out. "Right, Bob, I'll go get Jack to unlock the cellar door so we can unload the new kegs, and then we'll get the old ones onto the wagon."

"Right you are, Reg," said the other man, "We'd better get a shift on, we're running late."

"And don't I know it, eh? No time to stop for a pint today, and I'm parched too."

Frantically I pulled at Bella's leash, and we set off at a run, but not before the rather large package in Bella's mouth knocked against a tower of six kegs making them sway most alarmingly and, as we ran hell for leather, a tremendous crash rang through the air and a loud bellow from one of the men, "Good grief, all hell's broken loose here, Bob."

I took a quick peek over my shoulder, where I saw kegs rolling around, the two men frantically trying to catch them, accompanied by Jack the landlord, who'd come outside, a bemused expression on his face. As Bella and I approached the park, we slowed down a little, my heart hammered, and sweat ran in little rivers down my face. With a bit of coaxing (plenty of treats), I took the package from Bella's mouth and put it carefully into my rucksack. She smiled at me, and gave me the side eye, showing all her little white teeth as if to say, "Well, human, what do you think? Aren't I a clever girl?"

We walked sedately around the park, breathing in the fresh scent of freshly cut grass. I didn't see any of the other dog walkers or Michael Lawrence, which was a good thing as I certainly wasn't in the mood for idle chit-chat with him. That's if he spoke to me at all, after what happened the last time I'd seen him in the *Rabbit and Bear*. I still felt buoyed up, on a high, an adrenaline high, I suppose you'd call it, and the thought that I could have been carrying a human leg in my rucksack gave me the shivers.

Later, when I got home and gingerly opened the package, it was indeed a human leg, the lower leg including the knee, but with no foot attached. The clue read, 'Well done, you; you are good!' *You found the leg just as you should. Now look in the churchyard of our Saint John, beneath a widespread tree, the tomb of a man named Don. The clue is right there on the stone, to assist you in finding the bone!"*

I noticed that, just as the other clues, the letter "E" was at an odd angle and even more faded than the rest of the wording. Now, if only I could find out who had a typewriter with a dodgy letter like that, then maybe the culprit could be found. Carefully wrapping the leg up again, I put it in my rucksack along with the clue and, taking a deep breath, mentally prepared myself for the police station and the gorgeous, good looks, and perhaps anger, of Detective Inspector Jay Sutherland.

***

June 1972 – A Dilemma with Mum and Dad

"Hello? Hello? Who is it? Steph, is it you?"

The sound of gulping and sniffing came through the curly telephone wire and straight into my ear. My heart thumped, and I felt a mix of worry and fear. This person sounded so distressed. I said, "Who is it? Please, tell me. I can't help you if you don't tell me."

"Mandy?" There was a choked sob and then another tortured rendition of, "Mandy?"

It sounded like Mum, was it Mum? I decided to ask and said, "Mum?"

"Oh, Mandy!"

"What is it, Mum? Oh my God, what's happened? Is it Dad?"

"Yes, it is, it's him. *Your* dad." She emphasized the "your" as if he were solely mine now, and she wanted nothing further to do with him. A terrible cold feeling, as if a block of ice had melted from the top of my head to the tip of my toes, drained through me.

"Oh no, what's happened, Mum?" "He's dead," I thought to myself, "My dad's dead." I felt numb, totally numb and fully prepared for her to say, "Yes, Mandy, he is. I'm sorry to tell you over the phone," but instead, after a further bout of sniffing and crying, her voice wobbly, she said something unexpected.

"He's having an affair, Mandy?"

"What? Dad having an affair?" I felt laughter bubbling up inside me, "No, Mum, don't be daft, you must have got it wrong!"

"I am not wrong," she said slowly and carefully, "He's

having an affair, and don't you dare laugh, Mandy."

"I'm not, Mum, I'm not laughing. Look, what makes you think Dad's having an affair?"

I thought of my kind and gentle dad, always trying to please my mum. He wasn't what they call a "man's man." He didn't go out to the pub and come home worse for wear. If drinking was involved, he did it at home, in front of the TV, watching Coronation Street or one of his favorites, Mastermind; he loved to answer the questions, mum sitting beside him. There was no womanizing with my dad, he was a good husband and a good dad, come to that, the real deal.

"I'm pushing sixty, Mandy, and this is what he goes and does to me. I'm old, Mandy, I'll never find anybody else if he leaves me!"

"Do you want anybody else, Mum?"

"If he can do it, so can I, Mandy. I'm still attractive, you know. I've still got it!"

I sighed, "Mum, of course you are, but please, tell me why you think he's having an affair."

"He's been to the Rabbit and Bear a lot lately, always smelling of stuff, you know, that Hai Karate perfume and, well, he," She paused it seemed for ages, "He puts that Brylcreem stuff on his hair." She went off into a frenzied bout of weeping.

"It's aftershave, not perfume, Mum. Men don't wear perfume."

"Oh, don't be so picky, Mandy."

"That doesn't mean he's having an affair though, Mum, but" And here my heart sank, "Why is he going to the Rabbit and Bear? He never goes to the pub."

"Oh, he's joined their Real Ale Club," She gave a

mirthless laugh, "Just an excuse to meet women, I think."

"But Mum, Dad loves all the real ales, and anyway, you haven't seen him with a woman hanging off his arm, have you?"

"Oh, Mandy, what will it take to make you believe me? Okay, maybe this will. I found lipstick on his shirt, red lipstick. So, what do you say to that?"

"Are you sure it's lipstick, Mum, and not tomato sauce or something similar?"

"Oh, I knew you wouldn't understand. You've always been such a daddy's girl."

"But Mum, I do. Mum?" There was a long, painful silence, just the static burring of an empty line. She'd only gone and hung up on me.

Abruptly, I sat down on the settee, and my heart beat hard and fast. Okay, perhaps I could do with backup now, in the form of a brother or a sister, but then again, no. I'm possessive about my parents, as in they're my mum and dad, and I wouldn't want to share them. As well as that, though, as if I didn't have enough on my plate at the moment, what with trying to build up my business and the worry of finding the body parts and being, in a way, under caution by the police, albeit the very attractive Detective Inspector Jay Sutherland.

I also had a suspicion that Michael Lawrence was stalking me. Yes, a real suspicion. Thank God, Sophie, the mean Chihuahua was with me today in the park when I'd spied him from a distance. She'd growled deep in her throat as if she knew he was nearby, as if she could smell him or sensed him there somewhere in the vicinity. Okay, maybe it was just his Old Spice aftershave that she was upset about, but I was going to keep tabs on him, and if the stalking carried on, I'd go straight to the police and report him for harassment.

So, unfortunately, Mum would have to wait. I'd go and see her tomorrow, as I was going to be busy tonight in a very unexpected way. Read on and find out what I mean.

***

Earlier at Lambuck Police Station

We went to the same room as before, with the one high window and the cold radiator. Once again, we sat on the hard, uncomfortable chairs, the table between us, but with four body parts in a row now and not three. To sum up, this consisted of the hand, the skull, the top part of the arm, and the lower part of the leg.

"So, Mandy," he said, "You've carried on following the clues despite what I said, have you?"

I smiled; I simply had to. He looked as if he was mad at me, but the sound of my name coming from his lips sounded soft and caring, making me think that he wasn't mad at me at all, but glad I was there and that he found me cute and endearing. Oh God, I hoped I was right. And hoped that this time, he'd let me help him with this enquiry. I couldn't back out of it now; I was far too involved.

"Yes, I'm sorry, but this one was easy to find. Bella, another one of my dogs, found it, so I shrugged and said, "All credit goes to her."

He leaned forward, his forearms on the table, his face rather close to mine so that I could see the beautiful green of his eyes and a tiny mole at the side of his nose, oh, and the stubble on his razor-sharp cheeks and his chin. My heart thumped so hard; surely, he could hear it, yet he answered me calmly enough, "Oh, I see, well, you must thank her for me, eh?"

I smiled, not sure if he was being sarcastic or not. His tone indicated sarcasm, but his expression didn't, if you know what I mean.

"I have some news, actually, about the body parts."

"You know who it is?"

He shrugged, "Perhaps. We think they may belong to a woman who went missing approximately eight years ago, in 1964. A woman called Elizabeth Marks."

"Oh my God," I said, my hands covering my mouth, "How do you know that?"

"From tests on the skull," he told me, "From her dental records, we have an idea of age, we can gauge her sex by the size and shape of the skull, even her height. It's a difficult job, but we think it could be Elizabeth Marks." He paused for a moment and then said, "I'm trusting you with this information, Mandy. So, no blabbing to anyone, okay?"

"Oh my God, no, I won't tell a soul. But what about the other body parts? Do they belong to her?"

"It's difficult to tell, they're so decomposed. I mean, look at the hand, just bones, we can't even get fingerprints from that. All the parts we've found are just bones now, which isn't surprising and ties in with the length of time Elizabeth Marks has been missing.

He produced a piece of paper and put it on the table between us, "So this is the next clue, eh?"

I nodded as we both read it again to refresh our minds, *"Well done, you, you really are good! You found the leg just as you should. Now look in the church yard of our Saint John, beneath a widespread tree, the tomb of a man named Don. The clue is right there on the stone, to assist you in finding the bone!"*

"Well, what do you think?"

I looked at him from the corner of my eye, wondering where this was going, but said, "Well, there's a St John's Church in Tedford, but not in Lambuck, I'm afraid."

"Yeah, just what I was thinking," He glanced up from the clue to meet my gaze, "Are you up for it? Early evening?"

"Today?"

He nodded.

"Are you serious? I mean, after all, you did say that you would arrest me if I interfered again, that you had no choice. What's happened to that?"

He stared at me, his eyes narrowed, "I've decided to give you a second chance."

"Why?"

"Well, you seem pretty good at this. Could one of your dog's come with us? After all, they do seem to be playing a very active part in this investigation."

I nodded, "Yeah, maybe," as thoughts of an early evening walk with Sophie, the mean Chihuahua, ran through my mind.

A beautiful smile flashed across his face, "Okay, I'll pick you up then? What's your address?"

Not at all hesitant to give out my address this time, I told him it, slowly and carefully, just to make sure he got every number and word down correctly in his little black book. I left the station then, my head held high and walking on air, or what was it they said, "Better than Barefoot", just like the ladies in the Scholl footwear ads.

CHAPTER FIVE

June 1972 – Cracking the Next Clue

The beep of a horn alerted me, and I rushed to the sitting room window and peered out nervously. Sophie, the mean Chihuahua in my arms, snuggled up close like a baby. Yeah, okay, she might be mean sometimes, but when she's in the mood, she likes her cuddles too.

"It's him, Sophie," I whispered into her little floppy ear, "Oh my God, it's him. Detective Inspector Jay Sutherland was here, waiting for me, well, that's not strictly true," I narrowed my eyes, "He's waiting for *us*, and it's a miracle."

Heart thumping, I rushed outside and got into the car. T-Rex music played from the radio, reminding me of the two men, Bob and Reg, running after the beer kegs as they tumbled over and rolled along the road, *"Metal guru, could it be you're gonna bring my baby to me? She'll be wild, you know, a rock 'n' roll child, oh yeah..."* He gave me his mega-watt smile and said, "Hi there," and then looked at Sophie, "So who do we have here then?"

"This is Sophie," I said, "Also known as the mean Chihuahua."

He chuckled, "Yeah, well, they do say the little ones are the worst. Hello Sophie." Tentatively, he put out a hand to stroke her, but she growled, deep and low in her throat, even baring her teeth, so he pulled his hand back quickly, as a fleeting look of alarm crossed his face.

"Oh, wow, I see what you mean." He gave a nervous laugh.

"Give her time," I said, "And she'll get used to you."

"Mm, okay. Um, will she be alright in the car?"

"Oh yes, she'll be fine. Her owner takes her in the car all the time." I patted her little head as she made herself comfortable on my lap; her tiny body was warm and reassuring. The Detective Inspector nodded as if he was happy with that and started up the car, and drove it smoothly away from the kerb, but not before I'd seen somebody, or was it just a shadow, standing beneath the trees that lined the path. Oh my God, was it him? Michael Lawrence?

To control my rapidly beating heart, I said, brightly, "Oh, by the way, it was Sophie who unearthed the arm from the muck in a pigsty."

"Yeah," he nodded, "That's why I'm glad she's with us tonight. Who knows what we'll need to do to find the next 'bone' as it says on the clue."

"Do you think it might be a foot this time?"

"I don't know. Shall we see what's afoot, eh?" He gave me a cheeky wink.

"Oh, ha ha," I said, grinning, delighted at the Detective Inspector's off-the-wall sense of humor.

"Anyway," I said, "You look very smart for somebody who's going to be rooting around in a graveyard." He wore a dark suit with a shirt and tie teamed with shiny black shoes. I noticed he even wore cufflinks! Very up-market.

"Ah, well, that's because I'm at work, on official business, so to speak."

"Official business, eh? Who am I then? A concerned member of the public helping with an investigation?"

"Yeah," he nodded, giving me a side-eyed smile, "Yeah, a concerned member of the public."

I smiled as I gazed out of the window at the trees and fields teeming with sheep and cows that petered out to a more urban view as we approached Tedford. It was a lovely evening, the sky arching blue above us, dotted with fluffy clouds and a lemon sun shining.

I was acutely aware of the Detective Inspector beside me and the scent of his spicy cologne. I turned slightly so I could look at him. I watched his hands on the steering wheel; his nails were glossy and smooth, with no tell-tale yellow hue on the fingertips, making him, I would think, a non-smoker, unlike Michael Lawrence, who looked like he was wearing yellow gloves. He wore no rings either, not a signet ring on his little finger or a wedding ring, which didn't necessarily mean he wasn't married. My dad had never worn a wedding ring, and that meant nothing. Or did it now?

My stomach lurched as I suddenly thought of mum and the phone call earlier, and dad, my dad, accused of having an affair. It couldn't be true, but I would find out, oh yes, I would find out. A visit to the *Rabbit and Bear* on a Real Ale Club night was on the cards, that's for sure.

I put that business to the back of my mind; as my gaze returned to the Detective Inspector, then further up to his face, his profile mesmerizing with its straight nose and square chin, the green of his eyes standing out beneath the thickness of his brows. My heart beat hard and fast as I looked, unable to tear my eyes away, hoping and praying that the lack of a ring on his finger meant he wasn't married. The possibility of him having a beautiful wife and equally beautiful children hadn't occurred to me before; I don't know why.

His voice made me jump. "What are you looking at, Mandy? Have I got food particles trapped in my stubble?"

"Ugh! How would I know?" I said indignantly, "I'm not even looking at you."

He grinned, his body shaking with mirth, just as we sped past a sign saying, *"Tedford Welcomes Careful Drivers."*

St John's Church loomed in front of us as we drew up outside, its spire tall, pointing up into the sky; the graveyard teemed with gravestones, some at odd angles, like a mouth of broken teeth. Sophie trotted along between us, happy as Larry (whoever Larry is), a smile on her face and her tongue hanging out. She seemed to have taken a shine to Jay now, (as he'd insisted, I call him), despite her earlier hostility, *"Mandy,"* he'd said, *"Call me Jay, will you? Never mind Detective Inspector all the time,"* as she, with a fluttering of eyelashes, allowed him to put tiny treats into her mouth. She wouldn't let just *anybody* do that. Oh, no way.

We walked around the cemetery, the dry earth and leaves crunching beneath our feet. It was very quiet, as if a pall of silence hung over all the sad resting places. Massive Victorian tombs surrounded us, all ornate with intricate decorations and praying angels, their hands clasped at their hearts, the wording on the stones written in a flowing script. I let Sophie off the leash, and she began to potter about, sniffing at the earth and around the graves, her little nose snuffling like a piglet's.

"Have you noticed how many widespread yew trees there are in here, Mandy? This grave is going to take some finding."

"It doesn't say the tree is a Yew, though, does it?"

"Well, no, but there doesn't seem to be any other type,

does there?"

"No. Maybe we should split up and shout for each other if we find anything?"

He shrugged, "Okay. So, we're looking for a Don something?"

"Yeah, but I think it's more likely to be Donald, don't you?"

"Oh yeah, definitely more formal for a gravestone, eh?"

"Yeah, I think so, and don't forget, it definitely won't be Donald Duck!"

"Oh, you think you're so clever, don't you?"

I nodded and smiled as we moved apart, when Sophie decided just at that moment to do her "business," as we dog walkers call it. She squatted down between us, so I had to be ready with a doggy bag firmly in hand. Oh, the shame of it, the embarrassment at having to carry a bag of doggy doo da when the gorgeous Detective Inspector Jay Sutherland was with me. Sophie and I locked glances, hers with just a touch of mischief, and mine saying, "Oh, Sophie, couldn't you have chosen a better time?"

"Hey," said Jay, nodding his head, "There's a bin over there."

"Thank you," I said, hurriedly moving away to dispose of the offending bag.

"Hey, there's a Donald over here, Mandy," shouted Jay, "Donald Ferguson?"

"Hmm, I don't think it's that one, Jay, I've never heard of a bone called a Ferguson, have you?"

Laughter in his voice, he said, "What do you mean?"

"It says that the clue is on the stone, so maybe the

surname is a body part?"

"What? Like Richard Head?"

"Yeah, or Ivor Legge?" I said as I ducked down beneath yet another widespread yew to read a stone covered in moss and algae, the inscription hard to read in the darkness beneath the tree. It was cold here, and I shivered as if the dampness was seeping deep into my skin and bones. Sophie sniffed avidly, then yipped, emitting tiny, high-pitched yips and yaps that echoed through the still air.

"Have you got something, Mandy?"

"I'm not sure. I don't suppose you've got a torch, have you?"

"I certainly have. I'm on my way."

The leaves rustled, and he puffed and panted before he appeared beside me. "Thanks," I said, as I shone the torch onto the stone, the writing now easy to read. Sophie still yipped and yapped wildly.

"You've cracked it," said Jay, as he began to read, "In loving memory of Donald Angus Foote, born on 20 May 1901, died on 14 June 1947, not a long life, but oh my, what a surname."

"Ah, so there is something afoot, eh?"

Sophie dug deep, her little paws busy and her nose twitching, until, with her teeth, she pulled out a package. I took it very carefully, almost reverently, thinking of the poor Elizabeth Marks, and with gloved fingers, I removed it from her mouth. Muck and dirt fell from the plastic wrapping onto the ground where worms wriggled and spiders crawled. I handed it over to Jay, who, taking a bag from his pocket, popped it inside.

"Come on, Mandy," said Jay, as we crawled out from

underneath the yew tree, "I don't know about you, but I'm gagging for a beer. There's a nice little boozer that I know here in Tedford. Fancy it?"

"As long as there's a beer garden and a bowl of water for Sophie, then I'm your woman."

He gave me a smile and a nudge as we walked back to the car, saying, "Years ago, when I was a boy, I remember a lady called Elaine Body lived next door to us."

"So?"

"Just saying. It's a name but a body part, you know, like Foote, head, Legge. You know what I'm saying?"

"Yes, Jay, I do…how about Mr. and Mrs. Ear? Or Linda Knee?"

"No," he shook his head sadly, "Just no, Mandy…"

***

I awoke the next morning fuzzy and bewildered, wondering where I was until I realized I was at home, safe in my bed. Detective Inspector Jay Sutherland's handsome face loomed in front of me, and all the events ran through my mind. The foot (for yes it was indeed a foot enclosed within the package), Sophie's high yips as she'd pulled it from the earth and then in the beer garden, Sophie on her hind legs, begging for crisps, Jay's hand close to mine, and a half pint of cool ale called *"Frothy Funster,"* running down my throat.

Oh yes, I was a big fan of real ale now, almost on a par with my dad, so much so that I had thoughts of joining the Real Ale Club in the *Rabbit and Bear* so that I could keep an eye on him for Mum. But no, that was unfair, I didn't believe that Dad was seeing another woman. Not for a single minute.

All the same, though, I'd join the club for the beer; it was that good, but oh so very strong. Even the fruit ales had what you might call a sledgehammer hidden inside them. If there was a fight, say a Babycham in one corner and a half pint of real ale in the other, the real ale would win hands down. Oh yes, it would win the cup, take it home, and place it on the sideboard!

My dog walking for the day came to mind, making me wonder if I'd be able to live through it. Bungle, the service dog, was scheduled first at 9:00 a.m., followed by Max the Labrador at 10:30 a.m., and then Jessica the Border Collie after lunch. After that, I'd call to see Mum. There was no walk for Sophie, the mean Chihuahua. I'm sure she'd had more than enough of me after our adventures in the graveyard yesterday and her victory when she'd pulled the little package from the earth.

I closed my eyes and snoozed for a moment or two, my head deep into the pillow, content now that I had my day planned and that my thoughts were free to think about one thing and one thing only, Detective Inspector Jay Sutherland and the kiss we'd shared when he'd dropped me off last night. Yes, a kiss, dear reader. A kiss like no other, a kiss like none I'd experienced before or ever would again…probably!

But then disturbing thoughts drifted into my mind, thoughts that would have surfaced much sooner if it weren't for the effects of the real ale. We'd finished our drinks and were just about to leave the beer garden at the lovely little boozer called *The Hope and Anchor* that Jay had suggested. I must admit I was slightly under the influence, but I know what I saw, so here goes.

We were walking back to the car when I saw two people entering the pub: a man and a woman, their hands entwined like vines. The woman was nicely dressed as usual, long brown hair trailing down her back, platform shoes on her feet making her look tall and willowy, and the man, quite attractive at first glance but a miserable so-and-so when you get to know him, as I've found out only too well. Oh, yes, I kid you not, dear reader, the man and woman were none other than my best mate, Steph, and fellow dog walker and possible stalker, Michael Lawrence. So, just what do they think they're doing together, eh?

***

"You found the foot, I'm so amazed! Now go to a field where cows like to graze. There's a resident bull called Mr. Sam, lots of sheep, and sometimes spring lamb. There's fruit on the bushes and you'll have first dibs, look long and hard and maybe find some ribs."

***

I noticed a blackboard propped up outside the Rabbit and Bear advertising the Real Ale Club as I strolled past after walking Jessica, the border collie. Raucous laughter sounded from within as well as the beat of music pumping out into the street, *"Lord almighty, feel my temperature rising, higher and higher, it's burning through to my soul..."*

Curious and wondering if the Real Ale Group was in there now, I peered in the window, putting both hands around my eyes to shield them from the sun. *"Your kisses lift me higher, like the sweet song of a choir, you light my morning sky, with burning love..."* The bar was bustling, with people queuing two and three deep and sitting at tables, pints and half-pints of foaming ale in front of them. Cigarettes burned like little lights between fingers, smoke wreathing in the air.

My eyes searched the room, wondering if Dad was there, hoping I could give him a friendly wave and maybe even go in and join the group and tell them of my experience only last night with a half pint of real ale in *The Hope and Anchor* in Tedford. *"It's coming closer, the flames are now licking my body, won't you help me, I feel like I'm slipping away..."*

Disappointed, I turned to go home when suddenly, I saw him walking from the bar, his hands full, a pint in one and a half pint in the other. I was just about to tap on the window, excited, wondering if he'd managed to persuade Mum to join the club, too, despite her not mentioning it when I'd called to see her yesterday. I mean, after all, the half pint must be for her?

But no, he made a beeline for a table where a woman sat, a welcoming smile on her face, and a hand held out for her drink. Dad sat down beside her, and she leaned in to kiss his cheek. After which, he picked up his drink and took a sip. He sat close to her, their shoulders brushing, looking animated and happy as they conversed with one another. *"Your kisses lift me higher, like the sweet song of a choir, you light my morning sky, with burning love..."*

"Well, well, Mum was right then, Dad *was* having an affair. How apt, then, that Elvis just happened to be singing about "burning love" of all things. Tears threatened, and my heart beat hard and fast, and a frisson of what you might call rage shot through my body. I wanted to go in there now and shout at him, ask him to explain himself, but no, I held myself back, I'd only embarrass him and myself come to that.

Memories of my dad, just being Dad, came into my mind. I saw him as he ran along behind me, as he held onto the saddle of my new stabilizer-free bike until I had the confidence to ride it alone. When he put a fresh battery into my tiny Ingersoll watch just before it ran out, and when he always made sure I had a new needle on the stylus of my record player.

Nostalgia overwhelmed me so I had to walk away, my mind full of endless questions for Dad and just two questions for myself, "Should I go to see Mum right now and tell her what I'd seen? Or wait until I'd spoken to Dad."

After all, Dad and the woman might have been an innocent mistake, or perhaps I'd misinterpreted the situation. Maybe she was just a friend he'd made at the Real Ale Group. Apart from the kiss, the brazen hussy, a chaste kiss on the cheek, nothing pointed to it being a romantic encounter. I grappled with my thoughts as I walked my weary way home.

CHAPTER SIX

July 1972 – Discussing the Latest Clue

"Look, Mandy, I'm sorry about the other night. I, um, well, I was so taken in by your charms that I..."

"So, you didn't mean it then? The kiss?" Yes, I believe in being direct. It's the best way to be.

"Well, of course I meant it, but I was on duty and, well, it was very unprofessional of me."

"So, you don't want to kiss again?"

He laughed nervously, "Well, of course I do. Actually," He took a deep breath. "I'd like to spend more time with you, like this, going for a drink, and maybe, um, going bowling or something like that. That's if, well," He stumbled over his words, "You'd like to?"

"I would, but are you sure you would?"

"Yes."

"The thing is, are you in a position to see more of me and to kiss me like that?"

He frowned, "Position? What position are you thinking of?"

I turned to look over my shoulder. I didn't want anybody to be nosing into our conversation, did I? I lowered my voice, "You know, are you in a position to see more of me and to kiss me so passionately?"

Jay colored immediately, his face burning a bright red, making me smile. After which I asked the question, "Are you single? Or do you have a girlfriend or a wife at home? That question hasn't been asked or clarified."

"Oh, I see." He seemed relieved at being asked such a simple question, "Of course I'm single, Mandy." He shook his head. "I definitely wouldn't show my interest in you if I were married now, would I?"

"A girlfriend?" I asked.

"No, if I had a girlfriend, the same thing, I wouldn't two-time her."

My heart rose and the thought, "He's single, he's single," rushed through my mind, and yet a little demon still whispered in my ear, asking the question, "And yet, how come a man who looks like a Greek God is interested in you, eh, Mandy?"

We were in the *Rabbit and Bear,* sitting in a dark corner, just a sliver of sun shining through the tiny, ancient window and pooling on the table. I hoped no one would notice us, and they probably wouldn't as it was quiet in here, only Jack the Landlord, washing glasses behind the bar, and the inevitable older men playing dominoes.

Jay had a pint in front of him and I'd reverted to Babycham, a little afraid that if I'd drunk the real ale, it would go to my head and turn me into a weeping mess what with all this business with Mum and Dad and the burning questions I've yet to ask Steph after seeing her with Michael Lawrence.

I can't psych myself up enough now to confront either Dad or Steph, but at least I'm facing any problems with Jay head-on and trying to sort out one area of my life. Although really, we've come here tonight to look at the clue that came with the foot. The clue that's been going round and round in my head, the annoying clue that mentions cows and a bull with a name, sheep, and ribs, and doesn't make a lot of sense at all.

I took a sip of the bubbly Babycham before saying, "But…"

"But what?" asked Jay, a small smile lifting the corners of his mouth.

"You're, you know, so, um," I looked down at the table, "Well, I'll come straight to the point, you look like a Greek God."

He gazed at me wide-eyed, and then began to laugh, just a little at first, and then real belly laughs, tears forming in his eyes, "A Greek God?"

I nodded, "Yeah. Don't laugh, Jay. It's just that it makes me wonder, what do you see in me?"

"Oh, Mandy." He enclosed my hands in both of his, sending a lovely warm feeling all through my body, and said, "You're lovely, you've got beautiful shiny hair and bewitching hazel eyes, you're funny, you're everything I've always wanted," He shrugged, as if he was searching for more words, and then leaned in close to kiss my lips, saying, "My Goddess."

As if on cue, the jukebox sprang into life and The Stylistics began to sing, *"There's a spark of magic in your eyes, Candyland appears each time you smile…"*

It was my turn to blush now as Jay took my hand in his and, spreading it out wide, kissed the palm, the erotic feeling of his lips against my bare skin, sending shivers running down my spine, "Oh Jay," I giggled.

"So, have I answered your questions?" *"And betcha by golly, wow, you're the one that I've been waiting for forever, and ever will my love for you keep growin' strong, keep growin' strong…"*

"Yeah, but about this investigation. Is it okay that I help you with it?"

He nodded, "Yeah, of course. Hey, I'm the boss, what I say goes, but my team agrees that, as a concerned member of the public, you should play an active part, along with your dogs, of course. You've been a great help so far, once you brought the body parts into the police station, that is."

"Oh yeah, you were angry with me, weren't you?" *"If I could, I'd catch a falling star, to shine on you so I'll know where you are..."*

He gave me a sexy side-eyed gaze, making my heart beat more erratically than ever, "Yeah, for a while. After all, you were withholding evidence from the police."

The door suddenly creaked open, and a couple of young men walked in, making a beeline for the bar. They both had long hair and beards and both wore flared jeans and t-shirts, the words, *"Alice Cooper, Schools Out Tour '72"* written on them in big block letters, "Cor, I don't know about you," one of them said to the other, "But I'm parched for a pint."

"Yeah, me too. I don't know about one pint though, I'm gonna need three or even four!" They laughed raucously.

Jay and I grinned at each other as he took a piece of paper from the pocket of his jeans and said, "We need to crack this clue, Mandy." He spread it out on the table and we both sat simply staring at it, reading it again as a reminder of what it said, *"You found the foot, I'm so amazed! Now go to a field where cows like to graze. There's a resident bull called Mr. Sam, lots of sheep, and sometimes spring lamb. There's fruit on the bushes and you'll have first dibs, look long and hard and maybe find some ribs."*

"Have you noticed," I said, "the lopsided 'E'? It's the same on all the clues."

Jay nodded, "Yeah, I have. Any idea where that typewriter could be?"

I shook my head and sighed, "Unfortunately not, but it's something we're going to have to find out."

He nodded, saying, "I've seen a bull in a field just outside Lambuck, he's massive. Always gives me a menacing stare as I drive past."

"Is he called Mr. Sam?"

He grinned, "I'm not sure, we haven't been formally introduced."

I nudged him hard in the ribs, "Very funny. Hey, maybe if we go to the field and shout, "Hey, Mr. Sam," he might come running?"

"More like lumbering, due to his size, you know, but, yeah, nice one, Mandy. I think tomorrow we should visit him…"

"And the cows and the sheep, too?"

"Yeah, and I think there must be fruit growing there, too, blackberries maybe, and that's where we'll find our ribs."

"More likely to be raspberries at this time of year."

"Okay, whatever," He shrugged, "As long as there's a bull by the name of Mr. Sam, that's where we'll find our ribs."

"Ugh, I keep seeing spare ribs in a sticky red sauce."

"No, Mandy, the ribs we're looking for won't look anything like that." He gave me a cheeky wink, "Another drink?"

"Yes, please."

I watched him as he walked to the bar, marveling that Detective Inspector Jay Sutherland liked me and, oh boy, I knew just how much that feeling was reciprocated. Jay and I getting together was a dream come true, and, as well as that, it would shut up all those so-called friends who'd made narky comments about my clock ticking! All I had to do now was confront Dad and Steph, and my life would be back on track. Simple as that, right?

***

July 1972

I saw Steph before she saw me, coming out of the Providential Building Society, high heels tapping on the ground. She was smartly dressed as always, her trench coat pulled in tightly at the waist, giving her a fabulous silhouette. The weather had changed from bright sunshine to cloudy skies and spotty rain, so she pulled a poor battered umbrella from her bag and held it gingerly over her head, thus ruining her whole smart executive look.

"Steph," I ran after her, but she carried on walking quickly, her head bowed under the umbrella, as if she was going somewhere important, "Steph!" I shouted her name loudly until she turned around, a frown on her face.

"Mandy! What are you doing here? What's happened?"

"Nothing, I just need to talk to you. Have you time for a quick coffee?" The rain fell heavier now, in long silver sheets hitting the ground like knives, so, ducking under the umbrella with her, we ran, Steph saying, "Okay, just a quick one. How about Woollies again?"

Woolworths was packed, but there were a couple of seats at the busy lunch counter, which we nabbed straight away and sat down. Steph shook off the umbrella and put it on the floor in a sodden heap. We ordered coffees that came quickly, big mugs of froth that stuck to my upper lip as I took a sip, making Steph laugh. The smell of fried food hung in the air, along with damp clothes and damp hair, and all the windows were steamed up and running with condensation.

"Do you remember days like this at school?" asked Steph, "When it rained and we weren't allowed out to play, and the canteen was packed with us sweet-smelling girls and smelly boys?"

Laughing, I said, "Yeah, I do, and that mixed with the smell of school dinners always made us gag, didn't it? Thank God school is all finished with, eh?"

"Yeah, you can say that again."

I was just about to say it again when she fixed me with a glare and said, "No, Mandy, don't say it again." She shook her head. "Now, what do you want to talk to me about?" She glanced at her watch, "I haven't got long. I'm taking a half-hour lunch today. I've got a lot on."

"Yeah, okay. Look, Steph, I saw you with a bloke in Tedford the other night, going into the pub, *The Hope and Anchor...*"

She gave a great, beaming smile, "Oh my God, why didn't you say hello? I could have introduced you." She took a sip of coffee and said coyly, "It was our first date."

I took a deep breath, "I know him, Steph, Michael Lawrence, right?"

"Yeah." She looked puzzled. "How do you know him?"

I leaned in close to her, whispering from the corner of my mouth, "He's the fellow dog walker I told you about."

"What? No, Steph, Michael works at *Crunchy Crisps,* you know the crisp factory down Lee Lane? Are you sure it's him? He's never mentioned dogs."

"But he has a dog, right, Wilson?"

She shrugged, "Oh yeah, the big white fluffy thing? I saw him when, well…" She gave me a crafty smile, "When I went to his place."

Bewildered, I was quiet for a second or two, thinking, hmm, she went to his place after just one date, shocking, but then said, "Well, perhaps he works at *Crunchy Crisps*, now, but he was a dog walker. He's the bloke I told you about. I went out with him a couple of times, and he was very strange. I'm worried for you, Steph."

"Worried for me?" she said, as she pointed a finger at her chest, "Strange? Get real, Mandy, perhaps it's you who's strange! It seems to me you're just jealous. Have I stolen your man from you? Is that what this is all about, eh?" She pulled a silly face and then drained her coffee and put the mug on the counter with an angry click.

"No, it's nothing like that," I said, babbling, urgently, "I have a hunch he's got something to do with the body parts I've been finding. I'm working with the police now so…"

"The police? Have you lost your mind?" And then, "Quite the detective now, aren't you? Body parts indeed!" Deliberately, she looked away from me and then stood up, nervously it seemed, pulling the belt on her coat tighter, bending down for the umbrella, its bent silver spokes poking out from underneath the black material putting me in mind of a large dead spider.

"Don't go, Steph." I put my hand on her arm, "Listen to me, there's something not right with Michael Lawrence, and, Steph, I hate to say this, but I think he's stalking me."

She pushed my arm away, a look of disgust on her face. She said, "Oh, you are jealous, aren't you? Are you panicking then, about the clock ticking and all that?"

"No! I'm seeing someone, Steph, so that's not the issue, okay?"

"Seeing who?" And when I simply stared at her, "The Detective Inspector? Oh my God, you're seeing the Detective Inspector. That makes it even worse; even though you've someone, you're still not pleased that I'm seeing Michael Lawrence. He's a great guy, Mandy, a great guy, and" She paused for a split second, and then mouthed, "So handsome too."

"Mandy, of course I'm pleased, it's just that…"

Her look pierced my heart, and she said, "All the years we've been mates, and you treat me like this. Some friend you've turned out to be, Mandy."

I watched her leave, her walk angry, her back ramrod straight, long brown hair swinging. "Well," I thought, "That went well!"

I felt a tap on my shoulder and turned immediately, hoping it was her, my best mate, Steph, come to make amends, but it was a little old lady, her face hopeful, her finger pointing, "Is anybody sitting in that seat?"

I felt like saying, sarcastically, "Um, yes, the invisible man!" but instead said, "No, it's all yours," giving her a rueful grin, "And I'm going too, so you can have both seats."

"Why, thank you, dear," she replied.

I got up then and pushed my way through the crowded café until I came to the doorway, where I stood looking out, hoping that Steph was there waiting for me, but she wasn't. The rain had stopped, and a weak sun shone from a cloudy blue sky, making the paths and roads shine as if they'd been polished by a large hand brandishing a giant yellow duster.

With a heavy heart, I walked back through Lambuck,

hoping I hadn't messed things up with Steph. Despite knowing each other for yonks, we'd never really argued before, well, nothing serious, and her friendship was important to me. Perhaps I should ring her later, or maybe I should just butt out and let her get on with her relationship with the weird Michael Lawrence. But how could I, though? I didn't trust him; he was too volatile, likely to erupt like a volcano, and I'd never forgive myself if something happened to Steph because I didn't try hard enough to warn her against him.

I had to tell Jay I'd seen Steph with Michael Lawrence. He might know what to do, such as arresting him or taking some other action, but for what? For being a weirdo? Glancing at my watch, I quickened my step. I'd two more dogs to walk today: Jessica, the Border Collie, and my sweet little Sophie, the Chihuahua, who seemed to have undergone a personality transformation since she met Jay. I think she fell in love with him on the night we found the foot. Well, she's not the only one, eh?

Thinking about it, all I could hope was that my little "talk" with Dad would be more successful than my little "talk" with Steph. I couldn't imagine what I would say to him, how I would approach the subject. After all, he is my dad.

Anyway, I'd think about that later, or tomorrow. Yes, tomorrow would be far better. Because after all, tomorrow is another day! (No, I did not nick that expression from somewhere else.)

CHAPTER SEVEN

July 1972 - Meeting Mr. Sam and Cracking the Clue

T-Rex music filled the car, *"Telegram Sam, Telegram Sam, you are my main man…"*

Jay moved his body in the driver's seat, long, slim fingers tapping the steering wheel, and sang along, *"Purple Pie Pete, Purple Pie Pete, your lips are like lightning, girls melt in the heat, yeah…"*

"Shouldn't it be Mr. Sam?" I asked him, *"Mr. Sam, Mr. Sam, you're my main man…"*

Jay laughed, "Doesn't quite go with the tempo of the song, but good one, Mandy."

We sped along, Bungle the service dog on my lap this time, and Jay and I looking out for the field with the bull, the cows, the sheep, oh, and the fruit bushes, where, with a bit of searching, we should be able to crack the next clue. It was a warm, sunny day, with a blue sky, a yellow glow from the sun, and leaves on the trees a bright green, like the painting of a child fixed to the fridge door, highlighting the talent of little Bobby or little Jackie.

Jay pulled over into a passing place on the windy country lane and, craning his neck back, said, "I'm sure this is the field, but I can't see the bull."

"Maybe he's not out and about today," I said, "Worn out from looking after all the cows?"

Jay grinned, "Yeah, you could be right, but I'll tell you

what, let's find a proper place to park and have a walk, eh? We can see into the fields better, and I'm sure Bungle here would like to get out of the car, wouldn't you, girl?"

Bungle growled low and deep. She was in the early stages in her relationship with Jay but, I'd bet my bottom dollar, by the end of the day, she'd be eating crisps out of his hand in a beer garden, and falling in love with him, just as Sophie the mean Chihuahua had...oh, and me. Well, not the eating of crisps part, but the falling in love...definitely. That is, if a swift beating heart and a weakness in the knees constituted the real feeling of true love? But then, after all, the age-old question, what is love?

Yeah, okay, I'm getting a bit deep here. The next topic of conversation could well be, is reincarnation real? Or how did the Earth come to be? Or how many millions of years since the last ice age? Do you see what I mean? Anyway, let's forget about all that and get on with the story. Here goes. Jay found a lovely little parking area, and after retrieving a rucksack from the boot and hoisting it onto his back, we began our walk along the little country lanes. Bungle pattered along, her little body wiggling, the leash gripped firmly in my hand.

We passed fields of sheep and cows, their heads down, chewing on the grass, while horses snorted and frolicked, their hooves thundering on the dry earth. A breeze tickled the trees, shaking the leaves into a frenzy, and bees buzzed, and wasps snarled. Yes, wasps snarl! You've never seen a snarling wasp? Come on! Really?

Jay brought me out of my wasp reverie by saying, "Ah, now what have we here, eh, Mandy?"

I glanced to where Jay was pointing a finger and, to my surprise, there he was, the bull, Mr. Sam himself, a great big hefty fella, with a head as big as ten footballs, weighing God knows how many tons, but more than enough to break the massive scales I'd noticed people using in Boots the Chemist. His groupies surrounded him, an enormous herd of black and white cows, all with their heads down, chewing the grass, and ignoring him completely.

Gingerly, we took tiny little steps and walked closer to the hedgerow behind which Mr. Sam was lurking with intent. He must have sensed something or somebody because slowly he moved closer, and focused his little piggy eyes directly on us, and then threw his massive head back in a wild abandon as he bellowed, a bellow so thunderously loud it reverberated up into the sky and poor little Bungle stepped back, yipping and shaking in terror.

Jay and I exchanged glances as I said, "Somehow, I don't think we'll be going into that field, Jay. Especially with a dog! And how do we know the bull is Mr. Sam anyway?"

"It has to be, Mandy, and look, he's in a massive field, and look, right over there in the corner, I spy blackberry or raspberry bushes." He pointed his finger, "And they're a fair distance away."

"Yeah, but Jay, I bet our bull here can run like greased lightning. If he spies us across there with Bungle, he'll waste no time in introducing himself by getting up close and personal, and I doubt he'll be polite."

Stifling a laugh, Jay said, "Introducing himself? Oh, Mandy, you are funny."

"Yeah, I'm trying to be positive by making jokes, Jay, when really, I'm just scared. Come on, let's go."

"Go? What, abandon the search, and go back to the station without the ribs? We can't do that, Mandy." He stood still, hands splayed across his hips, his green-eyed gaze fixed on me. "What happened to your quest to help the family lay the body of Elizabeth Marks to rest?" He shrugged. "All forgotten?"

"No, not forgotten at all."

"And as well as that, what about the next clue?"

"Don't guilt trip me, okay?"

"Hey man, don't guilt trip me? What are you, a hippy?" He laughed dryly. "You started this, Mandy, you can't abandon it before the end. Come on," he jerked his head, "we can climb over the gate over there, right in the corner, well away from our Mr. Sam here. We'll find the ribs before he notices we're even in the field. And we'll probably be trespassing, so, if I were you, I'd be more scared of the farmer than the bull."

Reluctantly, I followed him and said, "Oh, is the farmer going to chase us at like one hundred miles an hour and boot us up the backside with his massive horns? I don't think so!"

Jay held Bungle, who struggled in his arms, yipping like crazy, making me afraid Mr. Sam would hear and come to investigate. As I awkwardly climbed the gate, moaning at Jay the whole time, I landed with a thump in the field. Jay handed Bungle over before leaping over easily like a true professional.

"You see," he said with a cheeky grin, "Nothing to it. Now quickly, let's have a rummage through the bushes."

He delved into his rucksack, producing a couple of pairs of latex gloves, and handed one pair to me before setting to work straight away, picking and poking among the bushes, his arms getting scratched by thorny tendrils. Half-heartedly, I began to help, keeping an eye over my shoulder for any signs of Mr. Sam spying on us and going off on a rampage. Bungle joined in, sniffing around the roots and the grass, her little nose dug into the ground.

I felt hot and uncomfortable, my skin prickling, the hair at the nape of my neck soaked through, and I wished I'd worn a hat. I also really hoped for a cool shower and a cool half pint of real ale or indeed a Babycham, the bubbles popping up my nose. I felt irritated and annoyed, my anger directed at Jay for making me climb the gate and for both of us, Bungle included, to be in this field with a mad bull and his harem lurking nearby.

Bungle suddenly began to bark, high-pitched squealing barks that echoed around the field. "Ah," said Jay, excitement in his voice, "She's found something, Mandy, look."

"Yeah, and the bull's going to charge if Bungle carries on barking like that."

"Yeah, but look."

"Oh my God, it's a bone!" I exclaimed as Bungle dropped it at my feet, "Just one bone."

"It's a rib," said Jay, "Good God, I expected a whole rib cage, not single ribs!"

He knelt beside Bungle, who, still barking, pawed at the earth, little puffs of dirt flaring up as the little dog dug deeper, revealing more and more ribs, until there was a huge mound, all of them black with muck. I gazed at them in wonder, "Oh my God, there should be twenty-four, shouldn't there? If they're all there?"

Jay nodded just as a loud bellow sounded out across the field, and glancing over my shoulder, I saw Mr. Sam, pawing at the ground, his gaze directed at us. The loud barking of the dog was stressing him out and escalating his anger. The whole harem of black and white cows stopped their chewing and lifted their heads, no doubt wondering what was wrong with their man. What had stirred up his anger?

Slowly but surely, Mr. Sam and the whole harem started a slow walk towards us, tails waving and heads moving up and down as they sashayed across the field, the same curious expression on all their faces.

"Right," said Jay, "Give me Bungle, Mandy, and get over the fence as quickly as you can."

With shaking hands, I handed Bungle over into Jay's waiting arms, only to stop mid-air when I noticed the mound of ribs, "Hadn't you better put the ribs in your rucksack first?"

"Oh my God, yes." He knelt and scooped up the ribs, stuffing them into the open mouth of the bag, trying to squash them all in. Glancing over his shoulder, his eyes wide, sweat dripped down his cheeks and chin as the bull, closely followed by the cows, picked up their pace.

"Quick, Jay!"

He just about managed to zip up the bag, shrugged it onto his back, and took Bungle from me, cradling her in his arms. At the same time, I leapt over the fence as Jay had earlier, a sudden spurt of energy catapulting me over as if I were competing in the high jump at the Olympics. Jay followed suit just as Mr. Sam bellowed again and began to run, the cows tearing after him, their hooves thundering on the dry earth.

We managed to escape by a hair's breadth, that's all, just a hair's breadth, Bungle still barking uncontrollably, mine and Jay's breathing short and ragged and yet, by a miracle, we were on the other side of the hedgerow as the bull and his harem came to a stop, hooves skidding, Mr. Sam's face was level with mine, his tiny eyes and flaring nostrils like a great beast from a horror film.

As traumatized as we were, we somehow managed to get back to the car, the sun burning down on us, even warmer than it had been earlier, with a yellow glow across the sky. Even Bungle was quiet now, subdued, and snuggled on my lap as Jay pulled away. We sped back along the windy roads to Lambuck.

"Do you fancy the Rabbit and Bear for a nice cool drink?" Jay turned the radio down, but I could still just about hear the strains of Don McLean singing, "American Pie," "*Did you write the book of love, and do you have faith in God above, if the Bible tells you so?...*"

I shook my head, "No, I want to go home." I glanced at him from the corner of my eye, "I have to take Bungle back anyway."

"What?" Jay turned in his seat to look at me, a frown on his face, "I can't tempt you to a half pint of real ale, or a Babycham? And what about Bungle? She'd love the beer garden."

The pub car park was quiet, only a couple of cars parked under the baking hot sun, but from the sounds of hilarity echoing through the air, the beer garden was busy. I shook my head, wanting to rouse myself from this awful mood but unable to, still harboring a resentment towards Jay because of the bull and the cows and the whole situation today. It didn't help that I was so hot and bothered, and sweat dripped down my neck and my back and between my breasts, and my eyes stung. I wanted to go home where it was calm and quiet and where I could be alone.

He sighed, "What's wrong, Mandy?" "*Well, I know that*

you're in love with him 'Cause I saw you dancin' in the gym, you both kicked off your shoes..."

"Nothing," I made to get out of the car, but Jay put a hand on my arm to stop me.

"Hey, come on. You can tell me, you know. I thought you'd be over the moon we'd cracked another clue."

I shook my head, "I am, I'm just tired, that's all."

"No, it's me. Something I've done."

"Okay," I turned to face him, his lovely face with those gorgeous green eyes and dimples either side of his mouth that appeared as if by magic, but I couldn't see any of that at the moment, my anger was so great, burning away inside me, "You put us all at risk back there, Jay, me, you and little Bungle here."

"Oh, come on, Mandy, we had to go into that field, bull or no bull, and we're okay, aren't we? Look," He spread his arms wide, "No damage done, yeah?"

"Yes, but I could feel the bull's breath on my neck, he was that close!"

"Well, we got the body parts we were looking for, and if they do belong to Elizabeth Marks, then we've got further proof of what happened to her, for her family, and then we're nearer to catching who did this terrible thing. That's our aim, isn't it?"

Sullenly, I nodded my head, "I know all that, but, oh, Jay, I'm making no sense now. I must go. I'll see you, okay?"

Opening the car door, I got out, holding on tight to Bungle. Jay leaned forward, his hand on the passenger seat. "Will you be in touch, or can I contact you?"

"Oh, I don't know, Jay," I shook my head, tiny little shakes, "Sorry."

Carefully, I shut the car door and walked away, heart thumping and sick to the stomach, as I hurried past the *Rabbit and Bear* and along the main street where I would drop Bungle off with Becky, his owner, and then go home to lick my wounds alone.

***

I awoke the following morning, unceremoniously pulled from sleep, by what felt like a heavy weight on my chest. I could barely breathe and panicked, hyperventilating, until I realized it was my sweet little kitty cat, Herman, in a lounging position, his paws tucked into his body and his clear green eyes gazing into mine.

Those green eyes reminded me of someone, and thoughts of Jay came crashing into my mind. Oh my God, what had I done? Had I finished the relationship? Absentmindedly, I stroked Herman's soft fur, feeling the delicate rumble of his purr, and wondering what I should do now. An apology would be the best thing, I suppose, but would he accept it? Was my apology worth accepting? And what about his apology to me for putting us in danger with that great bull, Mr. Sam?

With Jay, I couldn't help feeling he'd chosen me as a girlfriend because he felt sorry for me, and to top that his gorgeous looks made me feel inadequate and needy and the thought that I was too plain for him often ran through my head, despite what he'd said to the contrary. Hadn't he called me his Goddess? Despite that, though, my self-confidence had plummeted to zero, all because the man I was seeing was too gorgeous for his own good.

It seemed, therefore, that the key for me to succeed in a long and happy relationship was to let go of my Greek

God and find somebody else, somebody who was the total opposite, just as night is the opposite of day, and love is the opposite of hate. So, my new man-to-be is as ugly as sin and with the self-confidence of a paper bag. Voila!

And there wasn't only Jay to worry about now either, but Dad, oh yes, my dad, whom I'd bumped into last night just after I'd dropped off Bungle. My Dad, who had just been to his Real Ale Group, was walking home to Mum. The timing couldn't have been worse. I'd had a bad day anyway; the air was hot and oppressive, and I was in dire need of a shower and a long, cool drink. When Dad appeared, a great big smile wreathed over his face.

"Well, if it isn't my beautiful daughter. Come here, Mandy, come and hug your old dad." He held out his arms, but I side-stepped, saying, "Sorry, Dad, it's a bit warm for that, and, anyway, don't you think you should save that sort of thing for your lady friend?" Yeah, I know, I went in like a sledgehammer, not at all what I'd intended. I made to walk away, but dad grabbed my arm.

"Hang on a minute, young lady. What did you say?"

I looked him straight in the eye and said, "We know you're having an affair, Dad."

"We, meaning?"

"My mum and I."

"Your mum thinks that? That I'm having an affair?"

I nodded, a frisson of alarm racing through my body as he said, "Well," the smile all gone now, his evening ruined, "I've never been so insulted in my life."

My stomach dipped, but stupidly, I carried on, "But Dad, I saw you in the pub with a woman. She kissed you on the cheek. I haven't told Mum, though."

"How dare you," he said, and then after a pause, "You know, I never thought to hear such a thing from my daughter's mouth. Go on, away with you, our Mandy, go on away." He fluttered his hand at me but continued walking, his shoulders slumped, his old tweed jacket hanging from them like wings.

I stood stock still, "Dad, can't we talk about it?"

He didn't reply but just carried on walking, quickly and surely away from me, his whole stance hurt. I watched him go, my eyes filling with tears, so glad I hadn't told him that it was Mum who'd put the idea in my head in the first place. Maybe I'll ring Mum tomorrow and sort this out with her? Or perhaps leave it and mind my own business? And yet was Dad's inability to talk about it a sign of guilt? After all, I *had* seen him with that woman in the *Rabbit and Bear*.

Oh, what was wrong with me? I've upset three people now: Jay, Steph, and Dad. I'd be glad when this day was over.

CHAPTER EIGHT

August 1972 – A Shred of Hope

All the dog walkers were huddled together as if in a scrum when I arrived at the park with Max, the chubby Labrador. Their dogs, ignored for the moment, were running wild, smiles on their furry faces as if, with this newfound freedom, they'd surely died and gone to Heaven. Some squatted, their expressions determined, and yet there wasn't a single doggy bag in sight. My stomach sinking, I noticed that Wilson, the big white poodle, was there running riot with the other dogs, meaning that Michael Lawrence most certainly had to be too, and he was.

He was wearing his usual blue jeans and blue shirt, topped with a waterproof coat and even a beanie hat to combat the early morning chill. I watched him as he broke away from the group and strolled over. He raised his hand, as Wilson shimmied his way in front of him, but not before he'd noticed me, his mouth turned up at the corners in what I assumed was intended as a smile but looked more like the evil leer of the Joker.

"Yoo hoo, Mandy," Lydia, a tall, thin woman with a shock of curly blonde hair just like a dandelion clock, beckoned me over. I noticed that the whole group clutched a piece of paper in their hands, some reading it avidly. In contrast, others had it already scrunched up in their hands, as if to throw it away. I let Max off the leash. He went running off to join his pals, who were causing a doggy riot, barking and growling at everything that moved, including a poor little squirrel who, defeated, began to look for the only way out, a very tall tree to climb.

"Hi, Lydia," I smiled around at everybody, "Morning John, Judith, hi Liz, Reg…" Oh God, there are too many to name individually. They all gave me a nod and a thumbs up.

"Have you got one of these?" she asked, handing me the piece of paper.

"What is it?" I began to read, the words blurring in front of my eyes, *"Join me, Mick Lawrence, for a 'Real Ale' themed 40th birthday bash at The Rabbit and Bear on Saturday 23 September from 8.00 pm til late…"*

I didn't read any more for fear of a vomiting session being on the cards at such a thought, "Oh my God," I said, "I didn't realize he was so much older than me! A whole six years. Although a Real Ale party sounds fab to me."

Lydia grinned, "Got an invite, have you?"

"Um, no," I replied, "And I don't think I'll get one."

"Why?" asked Liz, a short, dumpy woman with a cap of grey hair tinged with a fashionable pink, "You didn't fall out, did you?"

"Not exactly," I told her, "We had a couple of drinks together, but, well, it wasn't exactly a match made in Heaven, if you know what I mean."

"He's a bit of a tightwad, isn't he?" put in John the wiry pensioner, "He's not even sending out proper invitations, just scrappy bits of paper." He looked at it with disdain before tearing it into four neat pieces and stomping off to a nearby bin.

A shaft of lemon sunlight suddenly appeared from the

misty sky, lighting up the park, illuminating the green of the grass and the bright primary colors of the playground, where screaming children shot down the slide like bullets from a gun and laughed, high and musical, as their parents pushed them on the swings.

In my mind's eye, I saw the invite again and asked Liz if I could have another look. She handed it over, and this time I saw it immediately—the dodgy "E" and the faded type, which proved that this invitation had been typed on the same typewriter as the clues. A dart of what felt like fear shot through me at what this could mean, and that my gut feeling about Michael Lawrence could be right.

I needed a copy of the invitation, not only to show to Jay, as part of my concerned member of the public act, but also to Steph. Hopefully, this could be the catalyst that would wake her up to the fact that Michael Lawrence was bad news. But then again, if she was still seeing him, wouldn't she already have an invitation?

The thought of Jay flashed through my mind and the familiar sinking feeling that I hadn't seen or heard from him in two weeks, six days, one hour and," I checked my watch, "two minutes." He'd taken my reluctance, on the day of the saga of Mr. Sam the bull, for no contact between us as gospel. I gave a great sigh before thinking that this invitation could well be the answer to my problem. It was evidence. Evidence that the police should see and evidence that I could take to them, ie, Detective Inspector Jay Sutherland. I turned to Lydia.

"Um, do you think I could borrow your invitation, please, Lydia?"

"Whatever for?" she asked, a worried frown creasing her brow.

"Oh, just…oh, you know."

"No, I don't actually. Not thinking of gate-crashing the party, are you? After all, just because you and Mick didn't get on at your pub soirees, doesn't mean he can't enjoy his birthday party."

"Oh no, I would never do that," I held out my hand, "I only need it for a while. I'll bring it back. I promise."

Reluctantly, she took it from her pocket and was just about to hand it over when a voice shouted, "Oy, Lydia, your Charlotte's doing her business. Got a bag, have you? Sorry, but I've run out; my Ted uses them up in the first five minutes."

With an "excuse me, Mandy," she shot off, pushing the invitation firmly back into her pocket as she pulled a doggy bag from the other one. Defeated, I tracked down Max, the chubby Labrador, firmly clipped on his leash, waved goodbye to all the dog walkers, and made my way across the park. I made a quick stop at the bin with Max's full bag when, like a blinding flash of light, an idea came to me. Hadn't John the wiry pensioner disposed of his invitation in this very bin?

I glanced over my shoulder to make sure nobody was watching, and delved into the bin, holding my nose with one hand, the other hand bypassing all the green and black bags, until I found them, yes, four pieces of paper, that I carefully folded together and put in my pocket. A bit of Sellotape and the invite would be as good as new.

In a hurry now, I rushed Max home and made my way to the police station to confront Detective Inspector Jay Sutherland. After that, a phone call with Steph was due. I had a lot of explaining and making up to do with two very important people. Oh, and that didn't include Mum and Dad, especially Dad. Well, not yet anyway.

***

The same Sergeant was sitting at the desk, a bored expression on his face as per usual, his lanyard still stating the name of Sergeant Tony Crawford. The waiting room was empty, just as it had been before, with not a soul sitting on the hard, uncomfortable chairs.

"Well, well, and who have we here then, eh?"

"Mandy Morgan," I said, "Um, Miss…"

"Yeah, I thought so. And what have you for us today then, Miss Morgan, a whole skeleton?" Standing up, he peered over the counter, his rather large belly preventing him from leaning too far, obviously thinking I had a large parcel with me full of bony body parts.

"No, no body parts today, Sergeant, but I would like to talk to Detective Inspector Jay Sutherland if possible."

Sitting back down and folding his meaty arms across his chest, he said, "Oh, you would, would you?"

"Yes, please."

"Something for him, have you?"

I nodded, "Yes, I have something that I think could be called evidence about the same case as before, and I'm bringing it in as a concerned member of the public."

"Oh yeah, hmm…" Glaring at me suspiciously, he picked up the phone receiver and began to press buttons, jabbing at them with his thick fingers, as if he wasn't pleased at all about any of this business.

I heard the click of the receiver as it was picked up at the other end, and the sergeant's voice immediately changed to a wheedle, "Detective Inspector, Sir?"

I heard a tinny response, and then, "I've a Miss Mandy Morgan here, Sir. Wants a word, she does."

Another tinny response after which the Sergeant replaced the receiver saying, "Go sit yourself down, he'll see you in a bit," And then as an aside, "When he's got nothing better to do, eh?" He gave a dry chuckle.

I shook my head and sat down on the hard, uncomfortable chairs, hoping that Edgar the drunk wouldn't decide to revisit the station while I was here. My heart racing at the thought of seeing Jay, the one and only Greek God, the minutes ticked by, tick, tick, tick. Just like my biological clock, eh? Tick, tick, tick. Through the window, I noticed the sun had gone behind pewter-colored clouds, and a welcome cooling rain had begun to fall, pattering down onto the now steaming, hot roads and paths.

I jumped as the door was suddenly flung open, and Jay sailed in, his long overcoat, over a smart suit, flying out behind him. His blonde hair flopped onto his forehead, perilously close to his snapping green eyes, and, as if a light bulb had suddenly been switched on, his smile lit up the whole room, illuminating every corner with his sheer gorgeousness. What had been wrong with me that day? Had I been temporarily insane to finish our relationship, and all because of a bull named Mr. Sam and his black and white harem?

"Ah, Miss Morgan, hi," he held out a hand as if we were passing acquaintances, and my heart sank, my stomach dipped and rolled. "How can I help?" His warm hand enveloped mine, making me shiver.

Taking a deep breath, I said, "I have some evidence regarding the Elizabeth Marks case that I think may be of interest to you."

"Oh, yes?" Imperiously, he held out a hand, "I'll take a look then, please."

My voice trembling, surely, he must notice that, said, "Um, well, I wondered if we could talk privately?"

He thought for a second or two, I could almost hear his brain whirring with all the pros and cons, and hopefully finding more pros, said, "Okay. Follow me."

He turned on his heel and strode towards the door. He held it open for me, just out of politeness, I'm sure, and we both went through and into the usual room with its one high window and cold radiator. We sat opposite each other, the table between us now empty, with no body parts on display. There was a long, uncomfortable silence, the only sound being the rain pattering on the grimy windowpane, before Jay spoke.

"Okay, so what have you got, Miss Morgan?"

"Call me Mandy. Please, Jay."

"Okay, Mandy, what have you got?"

"This," I pushed the piece of paper across the table,

He gave me a curious glance as he picked it up, and his eyes scanned the words. He shook his head, frowning, "A birthday invitation? That guy? Your fellow dog walker? The one you were with when I saw you in the pub?"

"Yes, but look at it, the invitation, Jay, it's got a dodgy 'E' just like the clues."

"So, the same typewriter?" He glanced up at me, his green eyes shining, and then with a frown, "Why is it all taped up?"

I chuckled, "One of the other dog walkers tore it up, in disgust it seemed, but I retrieved it from the bin. I don't have an invitation of my own."

"Ah, so he's shunned you, has he?"

I nodded, saying, "Yes, thank God."

Jay laughed as I said, "Guess what, I found out something else about Michael Lawrence, too."

Jay looked at me questioningly, "He's seeing my best mate, Steph. Well, he was up until a couple of weeks ago when I upset her for trying to warn her off him."

He nodded and said, "Yeah, people don't always listen, do they?"

I shook my head, "And also," I said, "I don't think he's a dog walker at all. He was always accompanied by his dog, Wilson. He works at *Crunchy Crisps*.

And then after a pause, "Well, I can't bring him in for lying about being a dog walker, but we can certainly bring him in now for questioning about the typewriter. Thanks for this, Mandy."

"Oh, I thought..." He cut me off by saying, "Can I keep this invitation?"

"No, I'll keep it. Can't we work together again?"

"I didn't think you wanted that anymore, Mandy. You said you wanted our relationship over, which is probably for the best."

"No, I didn't say that."

"Well, you gave an excellent impression; it was what you wanted."

"Yeah, I know. I'm sorry about that day, maybe I overreacted, about the bull and the cows."

"Yeah, and perhaps I did too, but..."

"Jay, I've missed you."

His expression softened as he gazed at me with narrowed eyes, making my heart thump hard, "I've missed you too. The times my hand went to the phone to call you, but..."

"But what?"

"I didn't think you wanted me."

"Oh, but I do."

He smiled his mega-watt smile, and dimples appeared in his cheeks, "You do? But that's great." He put out a hand to clasp mine, "Okay, but on a job, we must be professional, Mandy. We had to go in the field that day, bull or no bull. That's part of police work, even if you are just a concerned member of the public."

"Yeah, I get it. It won't happen again."

He squeezed my hand. "Friends again?"

I felt a sudden shyness as I nodded and said, "Yeah, friends again."

"Beer tonight?"

"Yes, please."

"Rabbit and Bear about eight o'clock?"

"Yeah, cool."

Jay sat back, his hands laced behind his head. He took a deep, satisfied breath, "Good, my life is back on an even keel again. Without you, I felt all at sea."

"Have you suddenly become a sailor and not a Detective Inspector at all? You know, even keel, all at sea? Ah, hoy, there, eh?"

"You are funny, Mandy." He sat forward on his chair, "Come here."

"Oh, before I forget. Was there a clue with the ribs?"

He shook his head, "No, there wasn't so, if that's all the body parts we're going to be able to find, it may be time to inform the family, and go to the press, it'll be on the radio, the TV." He held out his arms, looking at me expectantly, "Now, enough of that. Come here."

We stood up, and he pulled me closer and then closer still, belly touching belly, breasts pressed against chest. I looked up at him and cupped his head with my hands, pulling our lips closer and closer together until they touched, and I went straight to Heaven.

"I love you," he whispered, his breath tickling my ear.

I pulled back a little so I could see his face, and look into his eyes, "Really?"

He nodded, "Yeah, I hated us being apart." He shrugged, "I thought about you all the time. I love you."

A feeling of such happiness stole through my body that I knew without a doubt that what I was going to say was the right thing: "I love you too."

CHAPTER NINE

September 1972 – Michael Lawrence Interview

"Okay," said the Detective Inspector, as he switched on the tape recorder, "Today is Monday, 4 September 1972, Lambuck Police Station, Interview Room 2, and this is an interview with Mr. Michael Lawrence. The time is 3.00 pm. Present - Detective Inspector Jay Sutherland, Sergeant Leonard Hollis, and Sergeant Tony Crawford (Note Taker)."

I was going to watch in Interview Room 1 through a two-way mirror so I could see everything that was going on. Michael Lawrence had walked in, wearing his usual attire: blue jeans, a blue shirt, and a waterproof dog-walking coat. *Does he ever wear anything else? What a mess he is, and, really, what does Steph see in him?* I'd just noticed that he even had a black doggy bag poking from the pocket of his coat, which hadn't been zipped up properly.

Okay, yeah, I thought he was okay, but I was suspicious of him, right from the start. And I was right to be, as I found out for myself. To keep you in the loop, I spoke to Steph yesterday, but I still don't think I've managed to convince her of the danger posed by Michael Lawrence. She was blindsided and stayed that way, even when I told her about the same typewriter being used to type the clues that went with the body parts, as well as the birthday invitations. And, what makes it worse is she has an invitation of her own, and she's planning on attending the party.

Even when I said, "body parts," she doesn't bat an eyelid, as though she's under the illusion that they're not real, that they're made of plastic and we're simply looking for a mannequin. Anyway, I'd better listen to this interview. I don't want to miss anything, and it's hard enough to concentrate anyway with the distraction of the beautiful Greek God, Detective Inspector Jay Sutherland, in the room.

DI Jay Sutherland – Mr. Lawrence, I believe you recently distributed birthday party invitations to your dog-walking friends, whom you meet up with most days in Lambuck Park. Is this true, Mr. Lawrence?"

Mr. M Lawrence – Yes, I did. What's the problem? Can't a person give out birthday invitations now without being questioned by the police?" He gave a dry laugh, before saying, "Do you want to be invited, is that it? You're jealous, maybe?"

DI Jay Sutherland – "Oh, there's no law against that, Mr. Lawrence, but we're just checking out what you used to type up the invitations. You used a typewriter, yeah? Oh, and no, I'm not jealous."

Mr. M Lawrence – "Well, they were typewritten, so yeah, I'd say a typewriter was used." He giggled like a girl.

DI Jay Sutherland – "A typewriter with a dodgy letter and a dodgy ribbon by the looks of it, the types so faded."

Mr. M Lawrence – "Which letter would that be? The dodgy one, eh?"

DI Jay Sutherland – "The letter 'E'" Mr. Lawrence."

Mr. M Lawrence – "Well, I'm sorry to disappoint you boys, but the typewriter doesn't belong to me."

DI Jay Sutherland – "Oh my, well what a surprise. Of course, it doesn't belong to you, Mr. Lawrence."

Mr. M Lawrence – "It doesn't, okay?"

DI Jay Sutherland – *You know that we can search your house, don't you, Mr. Lawrence? And we'll find that typewriter, no problem."*

Mr. M Lawrence *(with a shrug)* – *"You're welcome, but you won't find that typewriter because it isn't in my house."*

DI Jay Sutherland – *"Well, where is it then, Mr. Lawrence?"*

Mr. M Lawrence – *"It's my mate's typewriter and it's at his house. He typed up all the invites for me. Saved me a lot of money. Money, I can now spend on real ale, eh?"* *He paused for a second and then said,* *"Oh, and I'll buy him a pint for his troubles, you know."*

DI Jay Sutherland – *"Mr. Lawrence, does your mate live in Lambuck?"*

Mr. M Lawrence – *"Yeah, he does."*

DI Jay Sutherland – *"What's your mate's name, Mr. Lawrence?"*

Mr. M Lawrence – *"Well, I don't think I can tell you that if my mate's going to get into trouble. Even you wouldn't grass on a mate now, would you?"*

DI Jay Sutherland – *"There's not going to be any trouble, Mr. Lawrence. We want to have a look at the typewriter."*

Mr. M Lawrence – *"He didn't steal it, you know. It's all kosher."*

DI Jay Sutherland – *"Stop with the rubbish talk, Mr. Lawrence. Just tell us the name of your mate."*

A long silence.

DI Jay Sutherland – *"Mr. Lawrence, a name, please. We'll sit here all night if necessary. There's no danger of that."*

Mr. M Lawrence – *"His name's Jason, okay?"*

My ears pricked up at that name, and I had a sinking

feeling in my stomach. I mean, just how many Jasons live in Lambuck?

DI Jay Sutherland – *"Mr. Lawrence, your mate's name, please."*

Mr. M Lawrence- *"Okay, Jason Rogan. It's his typewriter."*

I was surprised I didn't let out an audible, "Oh my God," but I did find myself covering my mouth; it was such a shock to hear his name in connection with this investigation. And yet, was Michael Lawrence being entirely truthful or implicating his "mate" to get himself out of trouble? Jason was a bit odd and a bit of a poser, but a murderer? Hiding body parts all over the place? I don't think so. But what was the explanation for the typewriter at that time? Was it possible for there to be two typewriters with a dodgy letter "E?"

DI Jay Sutherland – *Thank you for your cooperation, Mr. Lawrence.*

The interview is over today, Monday, September 4, 1972, at 3:50 p.m. Thank you, everyone. He switched off the tape recorder with a click.

***

September 1972 – A Clue is a Clue Wherever You Find It

The clatter of the letter box and the soft thwack of envelopes and flyers as they hit the doormat told me that the post had arrived. I rushed into the hallway, always excited when the postie came and picked up all the mail, shuffling through the contents (oh, to be so popular). As I went back into the kitchen, the kettle hissed on the gas. Herman, crouched over his bowl, eating his food with soft sucking sounds, a cute little snuffle thrown in now and then. The radio was blaring, and Tony Blackburn's voice rang out, *"Good morning, Radio 1 listeners, let's kick off today with none other than the great Elton John and Rocket Man. "She packed my bags last night, pre-flight, zero hour, 9:00 a.m. And I'm gonna be high as a kite by then...*

"Hmm, bills, bills, and more bills," I thought as I put the post into piles, the larger pile being flyers from all sorts of companies, flyers that I knew would go straight in the bin. Frowning, I gazed at the one letter that wasn't a bill, just a plain white envelope with "Mandy Morgan" written on the front in block capitals with a black pen, no stamp or postmark, so it had been hand-delivered.

Immediately, I rushed to the door to see if there was anyone about, like Michael Lawrence and Jason Rogan, for example. But there was no one there, no blue-clad figure or long-haired hippy wearing a biker jacket, just the street that I lived on, baking under a shimmering hot sun, the sky blue and no clouds anywhere to be seen.

I must have looked worried and afraid because the neighbor across the road, tending to his garden, waved and said, "You alright there, Mandy?" *"I'm not the man they think I am at home, Oh, no, no, no, I'm a rocket man, rocket man, burning out his fuse up here alone..."*

Smiling, I waved back, "All fine, Arthur," as I closed the door and, standing in the hallway, ripped the envelope open and pulled out a piece of paper.

"I watched you in the field with the bull. I don't know how you managed to keep your cool. Frightening stuff. Don't you agree? Never mind. This is the last clue you'll see. Now search in the allotment of your old man, dig deep and you'll surely find what you can."

"The clue," I thought, "The clue that should have been with the ribs. How odd that they've sent it through the post this time."

I read it through again, and again until it all clicked into place, the sentence *"I watched you in the field with the bull"* being the creepiest, and I imagined either Michael Lawrence or Jason Rogan, their beady eyes watching our every move in our antics with Mr. Sam, the Bull. The expression "old man" referred to my dad, so it was Dad's allotment. Oh no, how would we possibly dig deep in there? Dad would go ape if we ruined his carefully planted potatoes and vegetables and that's not even touching on the topic of his precious beds of dahlias and roses, oh and the great bunches of lavender that he nurtures solely for Mum, so she can make little bags of pot pourri that she uses to perfume her drawers.

(To clarify, I'm talking about a *chest* of drawers and not Mum's drawers (her knickers). You okay with that? Oh yeah, and I'm not forgetting the fact that I'm not Dad's favorite person now. Asking him if I can dig in his allotment will be a no, a big fat no, or even a no way.

"So, we won't ask," said Jay, when I phoned him a few minutes later to tell him about the final clue.

"We won't ask?" I repeated, "And you are a policeman? You mean you'd annihilate somebody else's property. My dad's property at that."

His chuckle, long and deep, echoed through the telephone wires into my ear, sending shivers down my spine, so I shrugged my shoulders. He lowered his voice, "We can go at night, under the cover of darkness, just the two of us, you and I."

"I'm not sure," I said, "You know, thinking about it, Dad is quite a believer in keeping on the straight and narrow, upholding the law, you know, that sort of thing, so maybe he will permit it if he thinks it will help the police."

"Yeah, as long as we don't go too near his dahlias?"

"Yeah, you've got it."

"And your mum's drawers?"

"Oh really, Jay, if you get hold of something with a minor sexual element, you'll try to milk it for all it's worth, won't you?"

His laughter echoed again, "You do realize I'm teasing you, don't you? Of course, we must get your dad's permission, and I was hoping you'd realize that."

"Very funny, Jay," And after a split second, "Oh, there's no dodgy 'E' on this clue."

The laughter stopped abruptly, "No dodgy 'E"? But there's got to be a dodgy "E" or we're doomed."

"Doomed?"

"Yeah! We'll need a new suspect. Oh God." I could almost feel his despair through the long curly lead of the telephone.

"No, Jay, we're not doomed. Jason Rogan will have bought a new typewriter, that's all. Don't you think? Michael Lawrence will have tipped him off."

"Yeah, you're right. We need to bring Jason Rogan in for questioning and then do a thorough search of his house."

"Right!"

"I'm on it!"

***

September 1972

"Mum, I think I've upset Dad."

"Oh, you have, have you? I wondered what was wrong with him. He's been like a bear with a sore backside for the past few days." I heard a sharp inhale of breath through the telephone line and knew Mum was smoking. Dad hated it when Mum smoked and told her often enough. Of course, she ignored him.

"Isn't it a sore *head*, Mum?"

"Whatever, Mandy. What does it matter, backside, head?" I imagined her shrugging, "Makes no difference. The crux of it is, he's been a miserable old so and so." More deep inhales of breath.

"I think it's my fault, then."

"What on earth have you said to him? I hope you didn't reveal our little secret."

"What little secret?"

"What I told you about," she lowered her voice, "That I suspected he was having an affair."

"You didn't say it was a secret, Mum."

"Oh yes, I did."

"Oh no, you didn't." Oh, good God, what a pantomime this was! Do you get it? Yeah?

"Mum, I asked Dad if he was having an affair, and he strenuously denied it. He was distraught."

"Huh, well, he would be, wouldn't he? He's been caught out."

"No, it's not that, Mum. It's all a misunderstanding, and I've thought about this a lot, and I think Dad's innocent."

She took a deep inhale and then a knocking sound as she stubbed the cigarette out. "You really should stop smoking, Mum."

"Oh, Mandy," She sounded fed up and bored, "You sound just like your dad. An old worrywart."

"Well, I agree with him in that respect. You should

stop."

"Look, Mandy, come for tea one evening during the week. All three of us can have a chat. We haven't been together for ages, have we?"

"Oh, okay. Can I bring someone with me?"

"Who?"

"A friend."

"Who?"

"He's a friend."

"He?"

"Yes, Mum, he!"

"What sort of friend?"

"Well, we're in a relationship."

"So, he's your boyfriend then."

"Well, yeah."

"Why didn't you just say that then, Mandy? Instead of going all around the houses."

"Sorry, can I bring my boyfriend? I'd love him to meet you and Dad."

"Yeah, but what if we talk about, you know…"

"The affair?"

"Yeah."

"It's okay, he knows all about it."

"Oh no, airing our dirty linen in public. Oh, Mandy, you do disappoint me at times."

"It's not like that, Mum."

"I'm still cut up about it, you know. The hurt runs deep, Mandy."

"Yeah, Mum, I know."

"Anyway, let me know which day you're coming, and I'll make your favorite."

"My favorite? What's my favorite?"
I don't know, liver and onions?"
"Oh, Mum!"
She cackled with laughter, "No, don't worry, love,
we'll send your dad to the chippy."
"See you next week, Mum."
"Yeah, see you next week, Mandy. Love ya."
"Love ya, Mum."
"Oh, before you go, I've kept that shirt, you know."
"Which shirt?"
"The one with the lipstick on it. I want you to see it for
yourself."
"It won't be lipstick, Mum."
"Oh, it is love."
"No, it won't be, Mum. Anyway, got to go."
"Okay. Bye."
"Bye, Mum."
"See you next week."
"See you next week."
"Bye."
"Bye."
"Have you gone? Mandy?"
"I've gone, Mum."
"Okay."
And then the click of the receiver.

CHAPTER TEN

September 1972 – Interview with Jason Rogan

"Okay, everyone," said the Detective Inspector, as he switched on the tape recorder, "Today is Monday, 11 September 1972, Lambuck Police Station, Interview Room 2, and this is an interview with Mr. Jason Rogan. The time is 10.00 am. Present - Detective Inspector Jay Sutherland, Sergeant Leonard Hollis, and Sergeant Tony Crawford (Note Taker)."

As before, during the interview with Michael Lawrence (also known as Mick), I watched through the two-way mirror in Interview Room 1. Seeing Jason close up for the first time in six months was a sobering experience. The handsome young rock God was gone. Yeah, gone, and so quickly too. Why?

Okay, he was still wearing skin-tight jeans and a biker jacket. Even so, he'd aged by at least ten years, not the good ageing of fine wine or a nice piece of cheese, but the bad kind of the deeply wrinkled face. He was also waving goodbye to his hair, as it had receded so far that the parting was almost at the back of his head, but the length of it rested on his shoulders. A shocker indeed.

Now look, I know a lot of men go through this, the hair loss I mean, but aren't most of them sensible enough to shave it off and be an attractive baldie? I mean, how about Telly Savalas and Yul Brynner? Both are gorgeous men with no hair. No, Jason's look isn't good now, and as well as that, he acted so disrespectfully, sitting slumped in his chair, as if he didn't care, his legs spread wide, and chewing gum, slowly, round and round like a cow chewing cud.

DI Jay Sutherland – *"Mr. Rogan, I believe that you are the owner of a typewriter with a broken key, namely the letter 'E'?*

Mr. J Rogan – *"I'm not aware of that."*

DI Jay Sutherland – *You're not aware of owning a typewriter that you used to type up birthday invitations for your friend, Mr. Michael Lawrence? As per this right here marked as "Exhibit 1?" Here, take a look.*

DI Jay Sutherland handed the invitation over to Mr. Jason Rogan.

Mr. J Rogan – *"Oh, those, yeah, doing a favor for a friend."*

DI Jay Sutherland – *"Well, you will see from the invitation that the letter 'E' is at an angle and the type faded, and this is your typewriter."*

Mr. J Rogan – *"Yeah, I can see that now, but I didn't think my typewriter had that affliction."*

DI Jay Sutherland – *"Affliction, Mr. Rogan?"*

Mr. J Rogan – *"Yeah, you know, something wrong with it."*

DI Jay Sutherland – *"So you didn't notice it at the time."*

Mr. J Rogan – *"No, I did not."*

DI Jay Sutherland – *"I think we need to look at your typewriter, Mr. Rogan. A search of your property will be carried out."*

Mr. J Rogan – *"You got a warrant?"*

DI Jay Sutherland – *"We sure have, Mr. Rogan."*

A short silence.

DI Jay Sutherland – *"Have you anything you'd like to tell us, Mr. Rogan?"*

Mr. J Rogan – *"Nope."*

DI Jay Sutherland – *Thank you for your cooperation, Mr.*

Rogan.

The interview is over today, Monday, September 11, 1972, at 10:20 a.m. Thank you, everyone. He switched off the tape recorder with a click.

***

September 1972 – The Hope and Anchor, Tedford

"Cheers," said Jay, as he clicked his foaming pint glass against my half pint.

"Cheers," I replied.

We were in the lovely little boozer that Jay recommended, The Hope and Anchor, the pub where I saw Steph with Michael Lawrence for the very first time, and where Sophie, the mean Chihuahua, ate crisps and flirted with Jay in the beer garden. It was a great pub, not as old as our very own *Rabbit and Bear* in Lambuck, but with a great atmosphere and a jukebox that plays up-to-date tunes. Exactly the tune playing now, *"They smile in your face, all the time, they want to take your place, the back stabbers (Back stabbers)..."*

"The O'Jays, yeah?"

I nodded, "A great song, don't you think?"

"Oh yeah," *"A few of your buddies, they sure look shady, blades are long, clenched tight in their fist, aimin' straight at your back, and I don't think they'll miss..."*

The pub was busy for a Friday evening, with numerous separate groups of men and women talking and laughing, mostly the women (isn't Friday night singles night?), and just a few couples sitting, holding hands or kissing in the dark corners. *"(What they do?) (They smilin' in your face) Smiling faces, smiling faces sometimes tell lies (Back stabbers) (They smilin' in your face)..."*

I gazed around at the beamed ceiling and walls, the long, shiny bar, and the real fire that crackled its way up the chimney, red and orange and gold, taking the chill off the dark September evening. Smoke wreathed in a cloud above our heads. I took a tentative sip of ale before saying, "Jay, how would you feel about having tea at my mum and dad's sometime next week?"

"Ah," He almost choked on his pint, starting a coughing jag, "Tea at your mum and dad's, eh?"

I patted him on the back, encouraging him to take another swallow of beer to clear his throat, "God, Jay, I didn't think you'd take it so badly."

Swallowing, red-faced, and patting his chest with a palm like King Kong, he said, "No, it's not that, beer went down the wrong hole. I'd love to."

I gave him a look, "Mandy, I'd love to meet your mum and dad."

I took another sip of real ale, this one called *"Ay Up,"* would you believe from the *"Dancing Duck Brewery,"* and at a mere 3.9% isn't likely to blow my socks off any time soon, "I thought we could ask dad about digging in his allotment, you know, explain the situation."

"Hmm," Jay looked worried, a frown creasing his face, "We shouldn't discuss the case with anyone else, Mandy. At least not until the family of Elizabeth Marks knows everything."

"I know my dad, Jay, he won't give permission until he knows exactly what it's for. We're going to have to confide in him."

"Does he know I'm a police officer?" He reached out and took my hand, rubbing the palm with the tips of his fingers, so shivers ran down my spine. "And that if I wanted to, I could get a warrant to dig the allotment?"

"Oh, you wouldn't do that, would you?" I wheedled.

"No, not if I can avoid it." He shrugged and sighed. "They might be a bit freaked out when we start talking about body parts and bones, though."

"No," I shook my head, "I know my parents, they won't be freaked out at all."

"Are you sure?"

"I'm sure," and when he looked doubtful, "Look, Jay, my mum showed me where the black hole of Calcutta is. It traumatized me for life."

"Isn't the Black Hole of Calcutta a dungeon in Fort William, Calcutta?" Narrowing his eyes, he gazed at me questioningly.

I shook my head, "Not in my experience, it isn't."

"Then I don't get it, Mandy." Slowly, he shook his head. "I just don't get it."

I smiled and said, "I'm surprised you don't have some inkling, but anyway, it's a conversation for another day. When you know me a little better." I drained my glass and put it on the table with a click, "Oh, and another thing. My mum thinks Dad is having an affair and wants to discuss it around the tea table."

"What? Oh no, Mandy, I can't be there for that discussion."

"It's okay, Jay, Mum knows that you know, but the thing is, I'm convinced Dad is innocent." I went on to tell him the whole story, leaving nothing out but telling him all the cold, hard facts. "I want you to be prepared, that's all."

"Okay, but, well, I'm not comfortable with that one,

Mandy. Digging for bones in your dad's allotment, yeah, but your mum talking to your dad about an affair, no."

Fed up with talking about it now, after all, how much could a girl take? I valiantly changed the subject. "Anyway, what about *your* parents. Where do they live? You never mention them, nor brothers and sisters."

"Yeah, well, my parents died a long time ago."

"Oh no, I'm sorry. How?" The jukebox started up with a crackle, *"In a little while from now, if I'm not feeling any less sour..."*

He drained his pint. "A car accident."

My stomach flipped with anxiety as he said, "I was in the car, the only survivor at eight years old, and, same as you, I'm an only child, so no brothers and sisters for me, I'm afraid."

"Oh, Jay. I had no idea." *"Looking back over the years, and whatever else that appears, I remember I cried when my father died, never wishing to hide the tears..."*

"It's not something I talk about really, you know," A small regretful smile passed across his face, "Anyway, come on, we're being maudlin, and we're not even drunk yet! Fancy another?"

"Yeah, and do you know what? I think I'll have a Babycham this time."

"A Babycham coming up, Madam."

"Do you think I should mix my drinks, though, Babycham with real ale?"

He shrugged, "Mandy, I think you'll be fine." He stood up and began to make his way to the bar, side-stepping and pushing through the crowds that stood three deep at the bar.

My heart swelled that he'd trusted me enough to tell

me about his parents, and then the thought, "If I hadn't been in the *Rabbit and Bear* that evening with Michael Lawrence, I might never have met Jay. So, thanks go to Michael Lawrence wherever he is at the moment. I raised an imaginary glass to him in a heartfelt toast.

***

"Exhibit 2," said Sergeant Tony Crawford, who'd been to search Jason Rogan's flat with Sergeant Leonard Hollis. Jay and I both gazed at the offending typewriter, a small blue and silver Olivetti. We're in the small interview room 2, with one high window and a cold radiator. The typewriter was on the table between us, along with the typed invitation, both marked with cards bearing the labels "Exhibit 1" and "Exhibit 2."

"It hasn't got a dodgy 'E' though," said Sergeant Hollis, "Nor a faint ribbon. The ribbon is dark and looks brand new to me."

"No dodgy "E?" said Jay dolefully, "It's got to have a dodgy "E."

"No, look." Sergeant Hollis took a clean sheet of paper and inserted it into the machine, typing something surprisingly quickly with one finger. *"The quick brown fox jumps over the lazy dog."* He ripped the paper out and showed it to us.

"See, no dodgy 'E" and no faded type. This is a new typewriter, Sir."

"Hmm, so he's swapped them, eh?"

"Perhaps, Sir."

Jay stood there, his voice firm and determined, "The original typewriter has got to be found, Sergeant Hollis."

"Yes, Sir. I'll do what I can, Sir. Unless, of course, this

is the original typewriter and somebody else typed those invites."

Jay took a deep breath, "Yeah, you could be right, Sergeant, but the dodgy typewriter has got to be somewhere. We need to find it, and fast."

The sergeant nodded, "Yes, Sir."

"I'm so disappointed," Jay said. We were standing outside now. It was a cooler day with an autumn nip in the air. "Feeling backendish," as my mum was fond of saying at this time of year. I was well wrapped up, though, and ready for the day's dog walking.

"Yeah, we need to find that typewriter if we're going to get the two of them, Jay."

"Yeah, yeah, Mandy, don't you think I know that?" he snapped. He looked every inch the Detective Inspector in his smart suit with a long dark overcoat over the top. Every inch a Greek God, as my rapidly beating heart was telling me.

"Sorry," I replied.

"No," He gave a rueful smile, "I'm sorry. Come here." He enveloped me in his strong arms, pulling me close into their safe curve. "We'll find it, okay?"

I looked up at him and said, "Yes, we will." And then his mouth came down on mine, his lips warm and soft, unlike the tepid weather, so I reveled in it, prolonging the kiss for as long as I possibly could until, reluctantly I broke away, coming back to the cold day and the cloudy sky, back to earth from my place in Heaven, "I have to go, Jay," I whispered into his neck, "I'm inundated with dogs today."

Gently, he let me go, "I hope those dogs know how lucky they are. Okay. See you tonight?"

I nodded yes and began to walk away when Jay

shouted after me, "Give my love to little Sophie, won't you?"

"Ooh, you are a flirt, Jay. You know Sophie's in love with you. Stop playing with our hearts."

He grinned, rolled his eyes, and raised his hand in a wave. I walked on a little and turned for one more glance, but he was gone. Gone inside to the warmth of the police station, to maybe look at the typewriter again, hoping upon hope, it would suddenly have a dodgy "E" and a faded ribbon enabling him to catch the culprits, so I carried on walking, my mind now full of dogs, content that I'd see Jay again that evening and I really couldn't wait.

***

"Mandy, Mandy," I turned to see Steph wobbling on her high heels across the park, "Wait…"

"Hey Steph, what are you doing? Shouldn't you be at work?" Sophie, the mean Chihuahua, started to growl deep in her throat.

"Hey, what's up, little doggo?" Steph crouched down and put out a hand to pat her. Sophie lunged, her jaw going down with a snap, narrowly missing Steph's fingers. Quickly, she pulled them back, laughing nervously, "Oh my God, is she dangerous or what?"

"Sophie," I said in what I hoped was a strict no-nonsense tone, "That's naughty."

"Oh, never mind, what's a couple of fingers after all. Look, Mandy, I'm in a bit of a rush," She glanced at her watch, "And I'll get killed if I'm late for work."

I shook my head, wondering what this obsession with getting killed by the Providential Building Society was all about. It was weird and downright unhealthy, to say the least. "Look, Steph, they're not going to kill you…they'd never get away with it…"

"Here, look, the invitation from Mick to his party. I thought you might need it as evidence. It's got the dodgy "E.""

"Aren't you going to the party?" I asked as I took the invite from her.

"No way, I've chucked him. You were right, Mandy, he's downright creepy."

My heart rose that she finally understood why I was warning her off. "What's he done, Steph?"

"Oh, loads of stuff, but last night he got angry with me. He shouted and, well, I thought he was going to kill me."

"Not him as well," I thought, but said, "Kill you?"

"Yeah, he put his hands around my neck, look." She peeled back her polo neck top to reveal reddened skin.

"Wow. Keep away from him, Steph, okay?"

"No way will I go near him ever again. You were so right, Mandy. Anyway, got to go. Oh no, there's a bus coming."

As she dashed away, her high heels dug into the soft grass, slowing her down. A smirk on the driver's face, the bus trundled past, so she raised her fist in the air and shook it like a maniac, only for another bus to suddenly appear, coming to a stop with a resounding screech.

I put the invitation in my pocket. "Come on, Sophie, let's play ball." I kicked the ball, and she ran off, little tail wagging, to retrieve it and bring it back to me, dropping it at my feet. And so, the game went on and on and on, my heart rising at every drop of the ball, at the thought that perhaps we could get Michael Lawrence now for something, even if it was only for cruelty to girlfriends.

My gut feeling told me he was mixed up somehow in

this business, along with his accomplice, Jason Rogan. Who would have thought it, eh? But then I had always thought Jason was easily led. All we had to do now was crack the final clue, and wasn't it outrageous that all could be revealed in my very own dad's allotment. Happy days, eh?

CHAPTER ELEVEN

September 1972 – A Visit with Mum and Dad

"Mum, Dad, this is Jay."

Jay, my very own Greek God, held out a hand and shook heartily, first with Mum and then with Dad. Mum had a sort of shocked look on her face, you know, eyes bugging, jaw hanging open, which didn't surprise me as Jay looked every inch gorgeous in his tight blue jeans and a t-shirt with some new up-and-coming band called Queen emblazoned across the front. I'd never heard of them, but Jay was obsessed.

"I'm pleased to meet you, Mr. and Mrs. Morgan," he said sincerely.

"Oh, don't stand on ceremony here," gushed Mum, "Just call us Angie and Steve."

"Stephen," corrected Dad.

Jay smiled his mega-watt smile, dimples appearing. "Good to meet you, Angie." He nodded towards Dad, "Stephen."

"Hmm, I hope you're taking good care of my daughter," said Dad gruffly.

"Oh yes, of course," stammered Jay.

"Come on, come on," said Mum, butting in as usual, "Let's go sit in the sitting room, our best room." She giggled as we all filed into the chilly best room that we hardly ever used, "I'll make coffee if you'd like some?" Memories stirred whenever I came into this room, its mural of mountains and lakes on one wall and three flying ducks on the other, took me straight back to my childhood days.

"I'll make it, said Dad, promptly disappearing into the kitchen, as if he couldn't wait to get away.

"He's such a modern man," gushed Mum, who, once he'd gone, furtively peered over her shoulder, before she delved into her bag and produced a packet of Silk Cut cigarettes and promptly lit up using the large silver lighter that sat on the coffee table.

She took a deep drag, after which she blew a long plume of grey smoke into the air. "Mum," I hissed, "Dad will go ape!"

Jay watched, his eyes round as saucers, no doubt fearing for Mum's life when Dad came back, carrying the tea tray, the door banging open, and all the best cups and saucers rattling as he put it down on the coffee table. Sniffing the air like a bloodhound, he said, "Are you smoking, Angela?".

"No, don't be daft," she replied, as frantically, she stubbed the cigarette out in a blue glass ashtray, leaving just a telltale whiff of smoke that spiraled around the room, which eagle-eyed Dad gazed at with disdain. He sat down with a great sigh, whilst Mum poured the coffee and handed the cups and saucers around.

"Mum and Dad," I said, delving in straight away, "Jay and I have something we need to talk to you about."

"Good God," said Dad, almost spilling coffee into his saucer as he sat up to attention, "Don't tell me you're pregnant, our Mandy!"

"Dad, get straight to the point, why don't you?" I shrieked, whilst Jay, the coffee having gone down the wrong hole, went into a coughing fit.

Mum started to laugh, and then, giving Dad a dirty look, said, "Pregnancy isn't always a bad thing, you know, Steve."

"I'm not pregnant," I said hastily, "It's nothing like that." I turned to Jay, "Jay, will you tell them?"

"Okay," Jay told them the whole tale, from the first time I'd gone into the police station with the skull, through to our adventure with Mr. Sam, the bull, right up to the latest clue which he read out loud,

"I watched you in the field with the bull. I don't know how you managed to keep your cool. Frightening stuff. Don't you agree? Never mind. This is the last clue you'll see. Now search in the allotment of your old man, dig deep and you'll surely find what you can."

"Is this a wind up?" asked Dad, his face blank and non-committed.

"No, it isn't, Dad. Look, one thing Jay has left out of his story is who he is. Tell them, Jay."

"What do you mean, who is he?" asked Mum, "He's not a murderer, is he? Oh my God, I need another cigarette." She reached for her bag.

"No, Angela!" spat Dad, "I forbid it."

"No," said Jay, at the same time dad spoke, his face concerned, "I'm no murderer, Mrs. Morgan, um, I mean Angie. We're trying to find out who is, though."

"Well, I'm suspicious," said Mum, red-faced now, "Who are you, eh?" She put her hands to her throat, her eyes wide, "Oh no, you're not Ted Bundy, are you? He's charismatic and good-looking, just like you. You could be his twin."

"Ted Bundy?" I shrieked with laughter, "Really, Mum."

Calmly, Jay replied, "I'm Detective Inspector Jay Sutherland from Lambuck Police. With the help of your daughter as a concerned member of the public, I've been working on this case, and it would so help matters if, as per the clue I've read out, we could have a look at your allotment, um, Stephen."

"This has got to be a wind up," said Dad, again blank, non-committed. He leaned forward in his chair and put his face close to Jay's, "No one goes near my allotment, lad, except one person and one person only, and that's me." He pointed at his chest with a fingertip.

"But Dad, this is important. You'd be helping the police as a concerned member of the public, like me."

"No way, Jose." He replied calmly, sitting back in his chair, settling himself into the cushions.

"Stephen!" said Mum, "Listen to Mandy, and don't be awkward."

Jay took a deep breath, "Look, Stephen, I can get a warrant to search your allotment, you know, although I don't want to."

"Oh, blackmail now, eh?"

"Okay then," I said, butting in, "This is getting silly. While you think about it, Dad, you know, helping the police, shall we talk about the supposed affair?"

There was a short silence before Dad said, "Supposed is the right word, our Mandy, and whatever you've been told and whoever has said it, it's a treacherous lie."

"Really," said Mum, quite determined now, "Okay, explain yourself, come on, Steve. Get it out in the open, eh? Who is your fancy woman?"

Dad checked his watch and then stood up. "Before

anything at all is discussed," he said, rocking back and forth on the balls of his feet, his hands clenched behind his back. "I'm off to the chippy to get our tea."

Jay and I locked gazes, as he too stood up, "Fancy some company, Stephen?"

"Um, well," Dad looked like a deer caught in headlights, his eyes skittering all over the place, but then, after what seemed to be a whirr and click of his brain, he relented, "Okay, you can help me carry them. After all, lad, four portions of fish and chips are hefty, aren't they?"

Jay grinned and said, "Come on then, my stomach's rumbling so the sooner we go the better."

They left then an unlikely pair walking through Lambuck to our local chippy. Jay was tall and blonde, wearing his cool band t-shirt, and dad was short with receding hair, wearing baggy trousers and a worn tweed jacket with leather patches on the elbows.

"Ooh, good, they've gone. I'll have a quick ciggie, and then we'll set the table, eh, Mandy? Will be nice for the four of us to sit together and chat, eh?"

"I wouldn't smoke if I were you, Mum, Dad always knows."

"Yeah," she said lightly, "The proper old ciggie police he is." And then carried on, "I'll tell you something, Mandy," giving me a sharp dig in the ribs, "He's a bit of a looker, is your Jay, isn't he?"

I colored up a bit at that, my face burning hot, so Mum laughed and teased me a little bit more, until I said, "Oh, Mum, stop it."

Well, I don't know what Jay said to Dad on the way to the chippy, but when they got back, he was all sweetness and light and gave his permission to dig in the allotment whenever we wanted to. So, Jay and I, with a little bit of help from Dad, have armed ourselves with spades and are now at work, digging deep into the earth to try to crack the final clue.

***

September 1972 – The Other Typewriter

"Sir, could I have a word, please?"

Let me set the scene. Those were the very words I heard as I walked in the park with Jay. He's off duty so had accompanied me on a dog walk, with Bungle the service dog who diligently walked between us, only stopping for a sniff in the bushes and the lifting of a leg and, even though I'm with Jay, my gorgeous boyfriend, I'm carrying a bag of doggy doo da with no embarrassment whatsoever. How my beliefs have changed since I started this job, eh? It's pretty liberating.

The voice, breathless now, spoke again, "Sir, could I have a word, please?"

I recognized that voice, that voice that sounded so mocking when speaking to me, but automatically turned to a wheedle when addressing Jay. Jay heard it this time, too, and we spun around to see Sergeant Tony Crawford hurrying along behind us, his belly jiggling inside his uniform. Jay frowned, "What's going on, Sergeant? I'm off duty, as you well know, and enjoying a dog walk with my girlfriend. Who's covering reception?"

"Sergeant Hollis is covering for me, Sir."

"Okay, so what's up?" He looked at him questioningly.

"I wouldn't bother you normally, Sir, but this is important and I'm pretty sure you'll be glad of the information. Sergeant Hollis agreed with that as well."

It was a blustery day, and leaves flew from the trees, their colors beautiful against the backdrop of a China blue sky, red and gold, russet and brown. Our sturdy walking boots shuffled through them, where they'd coated the grass like a multi-colored carpet.

Jay sighed, "Okay, but it better be good, you know."

"Oh," I thought, with a tremendous feeling of pride, "How manly he is."

"I found these labels at home, Sir. My daughter, Jennifer, is doing Domestic Science at school and…"

"Is that information relevant to what you're trying to tell me, Sergeant?"

"Yes, Sir. They're making jam, you see, in Domestic Science, and Jennifer has typed up these labels, you know, to go on the jars. Here, take a look, Sir."

Jay took the labels and scrutinized them carefully, his eyes narrowed. Peering over his shoulder, I saw immediately what Sergeant Crawford was referring to. Each label had a dodgy "E" with a very faded type.

"Good God," he said, "Wherever did she get the typewriter?"

"It took me a while to get it out of her," said the sergeant, "She's been wanting a typewriter for ages, but I said she had to wait until Christmas, and we missed her birthday, because…"

"Sergeant, where did she get it?"

"Well, she eventually confessed to having found it in a skip."

"A skip?"

"Yeah, the one round behind the supermarket in Lambuck.

There was only one supermarket in Lambuck, and we all knew where it was.

"Costalittle?" I asked.

"Yeah, that's it."

"Get the typewriter into interview room 1, Sergeant, and I'll be in to have a look at it within the hour."

"Already done, Sir, and ready and waiting for you."

Jay squeezed Sergeant Crawford's shoulder and said, "Thank you. Nice work, sergeant."

"A pleasure, Sir," said Sergeant Crawford, tipping his hat.

***

September 1972 – After the Fish and Chips

"Look, if you want to know the truth, our Mandy, then listen to me, eh?"

"Of course, Dad, that's all we want, isn't it, Mum?"

"Too right it is," Mum replied, spearing her last chip with some force, and putting it in her mouth, before placing her knife and fork neatly on her plate.

"Delicious fish and chips," Jay said, rubbing his stomach, "I'm full."

Dad nodded, "The best in Lambuck, lad. The very best."

Jay put the plates in a pile and collected the salt and pepper pots and the sauce bottles when Dad said, "Leave that lad, we can all sort it in a bit. Now, does anybody want a nice glass of my home brew?"

Mum made a funny face whilst Jay nodded, "That'll be great, thank you, Stephen."

"Mandy?"

"Yes, please, Dad."

Once settled, Dad began his story, "Now it's like this. My mate, Bert, is approaching his 70th birthday, and his wife, Rosemary," He turned to me, "The lady you saw me with in the pub, asked if I would help her arrange something."

"Yeah, but Dad, why were you with her in the pub?"

"She bought me a pint to thank me for my help in organizing the party, and, as well as that, she's a member of the Real Ale Club. Goes along with Bert, you see."

"Hmm," said Mum loudly.

"I'm quite friendly with Jack, the landlord at the *Rabbit and Bear,* so I said I'd have a word with him about hiring the room in the pub at a cheaper rate," He gazed around from face to face, "Being as Rosemary's only got her pension and that."

"Oh, my heart breaks," said Mum sarcastically. I gave her a warning glance, whilst dad carried on with the story, "After I'd had a word with Jack, he agreed to let the room for nothing, so it was a win-win all round and I got a free pint." He smiled around the table.

"And that's it?" I asked.

"Yeah, that's it." He turned to Jay, "What do you think of the home brew then, lad?"

"Cracking," Dad gave a pleased nod as Mum said, "Huh! So, how come you've been slathering yourself with that perfume stuff and putting that Brylcreem on your hair, eh Steve?"

Dad frowned, "Perfume? I don't wear perfume, Angela?"

"She means aftershave, Dad."

His eyes boggled, "I always wear aftershave and the

stuff on my hair. Good God, Angela, I wear it for you."

Mum wasn't about to give in easily, though. "What about the lipstick marks on your shirt, then?"

"Lipstick marks? What are you talking about, Angela?"

Abruptly, Mum got up and left the room, leaving the three of us staring wide-eyed at each other, giving me an opportunity I couldn't miss to regale Dad with a song, *"Lipstick on your collar, told a tale on you..."*

"Shut up, Mandy," said Dad as Mum came back into the room with a white shirt that she pushed into his hands as if it were tainted.

"Look, what's that then? I wasn't born yesterday, you know, Steve."

"I know when you were born, Angela," said Dad gruffly, "And it definitely wasn't yesterday," and then, after much scrutinizing and sniffing, "And this isn't lipstick, it's strawberry ale!"

"Strawberry ale?"

"Yes, from the real ale club. They're just experimenting with the fruit ales now, they're certainly not everybody's cup of tea, but the strawberry one does seem to be getting popular," Dad nodded emphatically, "What do you think, lad?"

Jay sniffed at the offending red marks and agreed with Dad that the marks were not lipstick but strawberry ale, "Lipstick's oily," Jay said. Mum, red-faced, looked down at the table and then glanced at her bag. I watched Dad watching Mum, with a funny expression on his face. He took a sip of his home brew and said, "Go on, love, have a ciggie, I know you want one."

Glancing at Jay, I said, "Do you fancy a bit of a walk?"

"Yeah, come on." He grabbed my hand, and we quietly moved away as Dad moved closer to Mum, and I heard his voice, "You know I'd never cheat on you, don't you, Angela. I love you."

"Oh, Steve. I've been so upset."

"Here, I'll light your ciggie."

"Thanks, darling, you're a star."

"Love you, pet."

CHAPTER TWELVE

Still September 1972 – Digging in Dad's Allotment

"Oy, watch me pom-poms," chided Dad, "It's all very well I've agreed to let you dig up my allotment, but you just keep your mince pies on my flowers."

"Mince pies?" asked Jay, bewildered..

"Eyes," I told him, "Cockney rhyming slang."

"Ah, I see," He nodded knowingly and then said, "Pom-poms?"

"They're a type of dahlia," roared Dad, "Don't you know your horticulture lad?"

"Not as well as you, Stephen, but don't worry, I'll be careful." Jay gave Dad a thumbs up and then carried on digging, his spade slicing in and out of the earth like a knife, worms wriggling to the surface, making me cringe. I'd just walked Sophie the mean Chihuahua, so she was here too, sniffing around the allotment and, much to Mum's amusement, "watering" Dad's vegetables with a lift of her tiny leg.

Dad, the supervisor, walked around nosing into everything, clad in what he called his "gardening attire," of baggy grey trousers, a grey shirt, even a tie, topped by a fancy waistcoat, which seemed a bit over the top to me for gardening but hey, each to his own.

"What was here before your allotment, Stephen?" asked Jay, gazing around. "Nobody else seems to have one around here, not even your next-door neighbors."

"This here," He spread his arms wide, "Was a ratty old piece of land that the council had neglected for a long time, so I took it off their hands, and bought it from them a few years after we bought the house."

"Ah, so that's how somebody managed to hide the bones here, then. They buried them before the land was your allotment, but that must be at least ten years ago."

"Yeah, sounds about right," and then, "Oh, what have we here then?" as Mum came tripping along the garden path carrying a tea tray complete with a plate of biscuits.

"For the workers," she said with a giggle, putting the tray on the wicker garden table and then sitting down, began to pour the drinks and entice us with the biscuits.

"They're shortbread, you know, come on, lovely shortbread."

"Pushing the boat out aren't you, Angela?" asked Dad, "What's happened to our usual Rich Tea?"

"Well, they do say that change is as good as a rest, Stephen."

"I see, alright, Angela, but I do like a nice Rich Tea, good for dunking, they are." He gave Mum a cheeky wink.

It was a lovely day, the sky was blue, and it was warm in the balmy September sunshine. I watched my parents, happy together again, and Jay, my Greek God of a boyfriend, and a dart of true happiness shot through me, followed by a stab of guilt and then sorrow at the thought of Elizabeth Marks, gone far too soon, and our sad quest to find her long-buried bones.

Ruining such a moment of enlightenment, Sophie, the mean Chihuahua barked, loud yips and yaps that echoed through the air, followed by a manic scrabbling in the earth with her paws, throwing great showers of dirt everywhere, and covering herself from head to toe.

She growled from deep in her throat and then became quiet and still, and despite Jay trying to push her away from the hole, she wouldn't move, and I had to resort to shaking a bag of treats to entice her away. Jay and I went to work, digging with our hands deep into the earth, and eventually pulled something out, something caked with dirt, dirt that we had to clean off to reveal the bones beneath. It was the other hand.

Mum shrieked and said, "Oh my God!" her hands cupping her mouth, as she caught sight of the bony claw.

"It's okay, Mum," I said, "It's a brilliant find, it's the other hand."

"That's handy," quipped Dad, unusual for him, as he always came across as being such a staunch, stiff upper lip type of person with barely any knowledge of jokes. How wrong could I be?

"There's got to be more," said Jay as he continued to dig, sifting through the dirt as if he was making a crumble topping, "I think there's some thick plastic here. Mandy, give me a hand, will you?"

Before I could move, Dad was there, Jay's right-hand man. He pulled hard at the plastic, knuckles white, until suddenly it came away from the dirt like a cork from a bottle, so Dad teetered on the balls of his feet, catapulting Jay backwards straight into a bed of Dad's dahlias, the plastic bag clutched to his chest.

"Oh no," groaned Dad, "You've flattened my dahlias, pom-poms, and all."

Jay groaned, "Sorry, Stephen."

"It's okay, lad, here, give me your hand." Dad pulled him up, and we all gathered around as Jay cut into the thick plastic and pulled it apart to reveal the bones inside.

"This must be everything now," said Jay sadly, "All that's left of Elizabeth Marks."

"Yes," I said, putting a comforting hand on Jay's arm, "But at least we can inform the family now. Its closure for them, isn't it?"

We all nodded, and Dad said, "Poor girl. Makes my flattened pom-poms seem unimportant, doesn't it?"

Dolefully, we all nodded, even Sophie the mean Chihuahua was quiet now, not a yip or even a yap or a growl as she lay cradled in Mum's arms, Mum gazing down at her as if she were a baby.

"Anyone fancy a glass of home brew?"

"Now that, Stephen, is a great idea," said Jay with a smile, "I've got a real thirst from all that digging. Oh, and look, your dahlias aren't flattened, you know, they're springing back up already."

"Yes," said Dad, nodding his head vigorously, "You know what they say, don't you, lad? You can never keep a good dahlia down." And with that, he turned on his heel and went inside to fetch the beer.

***

22 September 1972 – Interview with Jason Rogan

"*Okay, everyone,*" *said the Detective Inspector, as he switched on the tape recorder,* "*Today is Friday, 22 September 1972, Lambuck Police Station, Interview Room 2, and this is an interview with Mr. Jason Rogan. The time is 11.00 am. Present -, Detective*

Inspector Jay Sutherland, Sergeant Leonard Hollis, and Sergeant Tony Crawford (Note Taker)."

Once again, I watched with interest through the two-way mirror in interview room 2, dying to know how Jason Rogan would get out of this one. The typewriter with the faded ribbon and dodgy "E" must surely be his. He looked pretty much as he had in the last interview, wearing jeans and a leather jacket, his receded hair, long and greasy, lying on his shoulders.

DI Jay Sutherland – *"Now then, Mr. Rogan, we need to talk with you about your typewriter."*

Mr. J Rogan – (sullenly) *"Haven't we talked about that enough? You've got my typewriter. Went and stole it from my house, didn't you?"*

DI Jay Sutherland – *Ah yes, Mr. Rogan, but do you know what? I think you've been lying to us. The typewriter we found at your home was a virtually new Olivetti machine with a brand-new ribbon and not a dodgy "E" key to be found. So, we're just wondering, Mr. Rogan, how it was that you typed up those birthday invitations for Michael Lawrence with a different typewriter, i.e., the typewriter with a faded ribbon and a dodgy "E" key. Now, tell us all, Mr. Rogan."*

Mr. J Rogan – (sullenly) *"I don't know what you're talking about."*

DI Jay Sutherland - *"Oh, I think you do, Mr. Rogan, because do you know what? We found a typewriter with a faded ribbon and a dodgy "E" in a skip. The skip behind the "Costalittle" supermarket. A big old Underwood manual typewriter. This leads us to suspect that you, Mr. Rogan, disposed of the offending typewriter in this skip and brought yourself a new one, therefore thinking you were above suspicion in this case. But you're not, Mr. Rogan. You're* one of our main suspects, and until you tell us the truth, the whole truth, and nothing but the truth, you will remain one of our main suspects. Do you hear that?"

Mr. J Rogan - "Yeah, okay." He took a deep breath. "All I did was type up a few birthday invitations for a friend."

DI Jay Sutherland – "Oh yeah, and what about the clues, Mr. Rogan?"

Mr. J Rogan – "Clues?" He frowned, "What clues, man?"

DI Jay Sutherland – "Oh come on, Mr. Rogan, don't make me mad at you. Did you type the clues?"

Mr. J Rogan – "Okay, I typed them up for Mick, but it was just a bit of fun, a prank, he said. So that he could keep watch on that girl he liked."

DI Jay Sutherland – "What girl, Mr. Rogan?"

Mr. J Rogan – (eyes skittering, body shaking, even tears forming in his eyes). A dog walking girl. He liked to watch her when she found the body parts with the help of her dogs, but… (he began to laugh), they're just plastic. It was a prank."

DI Jay Sutherland – "That's where you're wrong, Mr. Rogan. The body parts aren't plastic; they are real and relate to a cold case from many years ago."

Mr. Rogan's head snapped up here, his eyes bugging from his head.

Mr. J Rogan – "Real body parts? Now you've got to be winding me up, yeah?"

DI Jay Sutherland – "No, I'm not winding you up, Mr. Rogan. Who is the girl Mr. Lawrence targeted to dig up the body parts?"

Mr. J Rogan – "Her name's Mandy. She dumped him, you see, so I think he was just out to scare her a bit."

A shocked tremor ran through my body at hearing

my name from Jason Rogan's lips (lips I used to kiss, ugh), and knowing that all this was planned and that I was being watched by Michael Lawrence, or perhaps the word should be "stalked." What's that saying? *"Who says a scorned man can't feel as much wrath as a scorned woman?"*

DI Jay Sutherland – *"I believe you also know this lady, Mr. Rogan."*

Mr. J Rogan – *"Yeah, I know her, but I had nothing to do with this. I just did the typing, you know. It was all Mick's plan."*

DI Jay Sutherland – *"In what capacity do you know Mandy, Mr. Rogan?"*

Mr. J Rogan – *"Well, she was my girlfriend for a while. Only four months or so."*

DI Jay Sutherland – *"And you didn't mind your 'friend' targeting your ex-girlfriend for such a 'prank' and scaring her? Or maybe it was you, Mr. Rogan. You who invented this whole prank to get back at your ex?"*

Mr. J Rogan – *"No, it isn't me. I swear it."*

DI Jay Sutherland – *"So why did you do it then? You must have known it was wrong."*

There was a silence.

DI Jay Sutherland – *"Well?"*

Mr. J Rogan – *"I didn't like it, but as I've said before, I just did the typing."*

DI Jay Sutherland – *"You're an accessory to the crime, Mr. Rogan, and will be punished as such."*

Mr. J Rogan – *"You can't get me for jack!"*

DI Jay Sutherland *"Oh, we can, Mr. Rogan, and we will. Now, what is the lady's full name?"*

Another silence.

DI Jay Sutherland – *"Her full name, Mr. Rogan."*

Mr. J Rogan – "*Mandy Morgan.*"

DI Jay Sutherland – "*Thank you.*"

Mr. J Rogan – "*Her full name, though, is Amanda Angela Morgan. I think Angela is after her mum.*"

"Did I tell him all that meaningless information when I was going out with him? If I did, God help us all."

DI Jay Sutherland – "*So to sum up, Mr. Rogan, you disposed of your old Underwood typewriter with the faded ribbon and dodgy 'E' in a skip in Lambuck behind the 'Costalittle' supermarket, and purchased a new Olivetti typewriter to avoid implication in this crime? Is that correct? And don't bother denying it now, your fingerprints are all over both typewriters.*"

Mr. J Rogan – "*Mick suggested it, but yeah, I chucked the old typewriter in the skip.*"

DI Jay Sutherland – "*Thank you for that, Mr. Rogan.*" And then, "*Okay, Sergeant Crawford, take Mr. Rogan to holding cell four, please. Thank you.*"

Mr. J Rogan – "*Hey, that's not fair. You can't hold me here. Innocent until proven guilty, right?*"

DI Jay Sutherland – "*Has it ever been said that life is fair, Mr. Rogan?*"

Mr. J Rogan – With a shrug, "*Well, no, but…*"

DI Jay Sutherland – "*Well, we can hold you here, Mr. Rogan, and we will. You're a menace to society.*"

The interview is over today, Friday, September 22, 1972, at 11:45 a.m. Thank you, everyone. He switched off the tape recorder with a click.

***

After the Interview

"We won't be able to hold him for long," said Jay,

"Unfortunately."

"But why?"

"Not enough evidence," He held out his hands, palms up. "As he said, he just did the typing, and was told the bones were plastic and it was all a prank."

We were in Jay's office now, Jay was sitting in his big Detective Inspector leather chair, and I was on the lowly one opposite him. "What did I tell you, eh? I had a feeling Michael Lawrence was stalking me, Jay. Oh my God, I feel creeped out."

"Yeah, I'm not surprised. I'm so glad I saw you that evening in the pub," He nodded his head slowly, his handsome face set, and his eyes burning bright green with anger, "I sussed him out then, you know."

"Yeah, I know."

"We're gonna have to bring him in again."

"I didn't tell you, but Steph came to see me the other day. She came to her senses and chucked him."

"Good for her, and about time too."

"Yeah, she said he attacked her, and she was scared."

Jay frowned. "Attacked her?"

"She's got marks on her neck, Jay. Like he tried to strangle her."

The phone rang, interrupting our conversation and causing us to jump. Jay picked up the receiver. "Detective Inspector Jay Sutherland."

There was a pause. "Sergeant Morley? Have you found anything?"

A tinny response and then, "Right, I'm on my way."

He put the receiver down with a click and said, "Sergeant Morley has been taking a little look around Michael

Lawrence's place of abode, and guess what?"

"Michael Lawrence's place? How? Did you get a warrant?" Jay was on his feet and making his way to the door.

"No. I sent the Sergeant to bring Lawrence in. He's not there, but the door was unlocked! Christ, you couldn't make it up, could you?"

Before I could speak, he said, "Now listen to me, Mandy. One of the rooms has a whole wall covered with pictures of you."

"Pictures of me?" I shrieked.

"Yeah, pictures of you walking your dogs, digging in the cemetery, running through the field pursued by the cows and the bull. It's all there, Mandy. All the evidence showed that he was stalking you. We've got him this time."

"Oh, Jay, so he was watching us. I knew it, I just knew it." Tears threatened, "And yet I felt so safe with you."

"Hey, don't get upset." He put an arm around my shoulders. "You are safe with me. I'm on my way round to his place now. Coming?"

"Yes."

He grabbed my hand, "Come on then, if he's there now, then we've got him."

My heart beating like a drum, I said, "Oh yes, Jay. I hope we can."

CHAPTER THIRTEEN

24 September 1972 – It's Party Time

"North side, east side, little willy, willy wears the crown, he's the king around town…"

The *Rabbit and Bear* was rocking, and the Sweet pumped their music out into the street, *"Dancing, glancing, willy drives them silly with his star shoe shimmy shuffle down…"* The air smelled of beer and sweat, and a mixture of perfume and aftershave, Estee Lauder's *"Youth Dew"* and *"Old Spice,"* at a guess. Huge puffy balls of smoke hung over our heads like barrage balloons.

I spied Mum and Dad sitting with another couple, and I recognized the woman straight away as Rosemary, the lady who had bought Dad a pint for helping with organizing this very party and who, horror of horrors, dared to kiss him on the cheek. The man must be Dad's mate, Bert, who looked cool wearing a trilby, a thin brown cigar hanging from his lower lip. Seventy today. Happy birthday, Bert!

Mum was talking with great animation to Rosemary, convinced now, by the look of it, that she isn't some sexy Siren out to turn Dad's head. I was eager to find out if Dad had persuaded Mum to join the Real Ale club instead of sitting at home, a cigarette burning between her fingers, and her imagination running riot that Dad was having affairs with all the women in Lambuck.

Grabbing hold of Jay's hand, I nodded my head

towards my parents, and he nodded back as we threaded our way through the crowd. *"Cause little willy, willy, won't go home, but you can't push willy round, willy won't go…"*

"It's our Mandy," said Dad straight away, jumping up to hug me, and then a handshake and a firm pat on the arm for Jay, and an "Alright there, lad."

"Try telling everybody, but oh no! Little willy, willy won't… go home…"

"Rosemary, this is my daughter, Mandy, and her boyfriend, Jay," Mum shrieked. She gave a saucy wink and nudged Rosemary in the ribs, "Isn't he a cracker, eh, Rosemary?"

"Pleased to meet you, I'm sure," gushed Rosemary, "Your mum and I are going to dance if you want to join us? Come on, Angie."

"Thanks, but I'll sit this one out," I told them as she grabbed hold of Mum and they both staggered onto the dance floor where they waved their arms about and sang along to the music, *"Uptown, downtown, little Willy, Willy drives them wild with his run-around style…"*

"I'll go and get a drink," said Jay, "What do you fancy?"

"Babycham, please, Jay."

I watched him as he bent down to ask Dad and Bert, "What's your poison then, you two?" My lovely Greek God, not only good-looking but generous too. I'd just sat down in Mum's empty place when I felt a tap on my shoulder and a voice said, "Where's Michael Lawrence then, eh? I thought it was his party tonight? His 40th."

I glanced over my shoulder to see a face I hardly recognized because of the heavy eyeliner and thick red lipstick. However, her hair gave her away —a great big, wild dandelion clock of hair. I realized it was Lydia, one of the dog walkers from the park, and the lady who had accused me of planning to gate crash Michael Lawrence's party because I'd asked to borrow her invitation, not having one of my own. I remembered her comment about a "pub soiree," which had made me laugh at the time.

I noticed the other dog walkers standing behind her, even John the wiry pensioner, all holding pints of real ale, yet with discontented, and even angry, looks on their faces.

"We've bought him presents too," said a tiny lady called Mona, holding up a little bag tied with a yellow bow and a tag no doubt expressing her love for Mick, as they all call him. Rumor had it that a few years ago, Mona was dragged across the park by Wallis, a massive husky, his sheer strength being too much for her to handle. It was well known that she now stuck to smaller dogs, like Bungle and Sophie, the mean Chihuahua.

"It must be in the other bar," I told them, not wanting to say the absolute truth that Michael Lawrence had gone missing, disappeared in a puff of smoke. "This is a different party, Bert's 70th."

"I thought everybody looked old," she said, looking down her rather long nose as she gazed around with disdain, no doubt feeling superior to all the old wrinklies who were bopping about on the dance floor.

"Seventy's the new forty," I said coldly.

"What's the new forty then, a teenager?" She gave an inane giggle.

"Probably, yes."

"Nothing is going on in the other bar, you know. It's virtually empty. Just a chap crying in the corner. We assumed you'd sabotaged the party because you didn't get an invite."

I was aware that Jay had come back and was sitting down next to me, a tray containing the drinks on the table. With a nod to him, I took a sip of the Babycham, hoping it would help to still my erratically beating heart. I felt such rage at what she'd just said, but replied brightly, "I didn't want an invite, Lydia."

"Huh, I think you did," she nodded knowingly.

Even more riled up, I said, "Actually I'd rather eat a large bag of doggy doo da than go to Michael Lawrence's party. Now, if you'll excuse me." Pointedly, I turned back to Jay, as an exclamation of "Oh really, how rude," echoed in my ears, and said, "Will Jason Rogan still be locked up?"

"No, unfortunately, he'll be out now, why?"

"I don't know, I've just got a gut feeling that he's the person crying in the other bar. I'm going to take a look."

He took a sip of his pint, temporarily distracting me as I watched his tongue lick the foam from his lips, "Crying in the other bar? Why would Jason Rogan be crying in the other bar? Have you finally lost it, Mandy?"

"I've just got a feeling it's him, and with Michael Lawrence nowhere to be found, he might have some information. There's no harm checking it out, is there?"

Jay and I stood up just as the DJ began to speak, *"Hey everyone, as you all know, we're here tonight to celebrate Bert's birthday. Please join us in a round of applause for Bert on his 70th birthday. Oh, my goodness, and isn't he doing well! Let's have a bit of Slade, eh? Come on, Bert, get that woman of yours on the dance floor! Seventy's the new forty, you know!"*

"I won't laugh at you when you boo-hoo-hoo coz I luv you, I can turn my back on the things you lack coz I luv you…"

The music faded a little as Jay and I went into the other almost deserted bar, the only people in there the huddle of dog walkers who gazed at Jay and I as if we were two headed monsters as we walked in carrying our drinks, and, yes, they were right, a poor bloke was crying in the corner, but he wasn't alone now. Jack the landlord was with him, hovering around the table, ill at ease, a look of relief on his face when he saw me and Jay.

"I can't get anything out of him. Maybe you two will do better."

"*You get me in a spot and smile the smile you got and I luv you, you make me out a clown then you put me down I still luv you ...*"

"Jason?" *Was this the gorgeous hunk of a man I'd cried over just a few months ago?*

He lifted his head immediately and gazed at me, watery-eyed. I recoiled as I noticed the blood on his face and hands. His pint mug was covered in it.

"What on earth have you done, mate?" asked Jay.

He burst into more sobs and, picking up his pint, took a sip. I noticed blood oozed from the cuts on his hands.

"Jason, you need to go to the hospital. Who did this to you?"

"I'd guess Michael Lawrence?" said Jay.

"Do you mean Mick Lawrence?" said Jack the landlord, "He booked a party here tonight and hasn't even bothered to turn up. What a waste of time, eh?"

"Yeah, well..." Jay began, only to be cut off.

"I hope he didn't hurt you like that on my premises," said Jack the landlord, giving Jason a look.

"No," Jason shook his head, "It didn't happen here."

"What happened then, Jason?" I asked, giving him a tentative pat on the shoulder.

He sniffed and snuffled like Sophie the mean Chihuahua when she begged for a treat, and then said, "He jumped me and made me tell him what happened at the police station. I told him everything I'd said, and he got furious and went at me with a knife. I stood no chance."

"Where did you see him? Nobody can find him now. He's done a disappearing act."

"Yeah," said Jay, "And when he's found, he's in big trouble."

Jason took a great sniff and wiped his nose on the sleeve of his leather jacket, smearing blood all over his face. "I was on my way here, to his party."

"So, he hijacked you, eh?"

"Yeah," He drained his pint, "I've never been so scared." Music echoed faintly from the party next door, reminding me of the day in the field with the cows and the bull, *"Telegram Sam, Telegram Sam, I am your main man..."* "I'd have been better off if you'd kept me locked up, wouldn't I?"

We chuckled mirthlessly, and a shiver ran through me as a sudden picture of Michael Lawrence's spare room came into my mind, and the wall that was covered with pictures of me. My ugly mug on full display. How embarrassing. He must have been watching us every step of the way, even being aware of Jay's rank of Detective Inspector as well. Did he think he was above the law? And how come I hadn't seen him every time lurking about, a shadow in the background?" *"Purple Pie Pete, Purple Pie Pete, your lips are like lightning, girls melt in the heat, yeah..."*

"What a mess all this is," said Jack the landlord, and

then rubbing his hands together, "I'll tell you what, I'll treat you all to a drink. Wait there."

He moved away, his progress to the bar closely monitored by the dog walking crowd, Lydia particularly, who eyed him up and down, her nose in the air as per usual, her lips pressed tightly together, as he poured pints and grabbed a Babycham from the shelf.

"Here you are then," and when Jay went into his pocket, "No, it's on the house."

"Hey, cheers Jack," We all raised our glasses, Jason included, who seemed to have come round a bit and even smiled, albeit painfully, his skin pulling at the cuts on his face.

"Jason," Jack the landlord, indicating with his head, said, "I've got a first aid box round the back. When you've had your drink, I'll patch you up a bit, okay?"

Jason nodded. "Yeah, thanks, Jack, but look," he said, showing him his hands. "The cuts aren't deep, and the bleeding has almost stopped."

"Alright for some, isn't it?" shouted John the wiry pensioner, "Come into a pub looking like you've been to hell and back, and you get a free pint."

"Not a good look, is it?" commented George, Gina the Labrador's walker.

"Come on now, come on now," said Jack the landlord, "You lot finished, have you? Ready for your next round?" He made his way behind the bar.

Jay slowly shook his head, "A bunch of troublemakers if you ask me."

"I'd like to see their faces when they find out who you are, Jay?" I took a sip of Babycham, the bubbles popping up my nose.

"Yeah, well, I won't forget them, but I'm off duty at the moment, Mandy, so don't breathe a word." He winked and put a finger to his lips.

Jason suddenly spoke, making us jump, "I wonder where he's gone then? You know, Mick. I suppose he might be back at home by now, though."

"We've no idea, Jason," Jay shrugged, "Have you any ideas? Any places he liked to go to?"

"Nah." He fumbled around in his pocket and produced a packet of cigarettes, and put one between his lips. He lit it with a match and took a deep drag, blowing out the smoke in a long, grey funnel. "The only place he liked to go was here, the pub. Loved it, he did. Always getting smashed."

"I wonder if his dog's okay?" I asked him, "Do you know anything about Wilson?"

"Yeah, a lovely pooch. Don't know why he loves Mick so much, though." He grinned and I could see just a vestige of that handsome young man I was so in love with only a few months before, "Animals are amazing, aren't they? But trusting, too trusting, I think." And then after a bit of thought, "Mick liked the park as well. Maybe he's gone there."

"Yeah, he might have liked the park for walking his dog," pointed out Jay, "But it would be difficult for him to hide in there, wouldn't it?"

"Wait a minute," I said, looking from Jay to Jason, "He told me once of a place he loved. He was born there, apparently, and spent his childhood there. They had a big house, um, now what was it called?" I was transported back to the day Michael Lawrence and I had gone dog walking, and he had told me about a place he loved, somewhere by the sea. "It's by the sea, I think."

Both men looked at me, frowns marring their faces. Faint music still sounded from the party next door. Then the sound of the DJ's voice, uproarious laughter, and singing, "Happy birthday to you, happy birthday to you, happy birthday dear Bert, happy birthday to you..." Everybody cheered, and then, "Come on Bert, the bumps, the bumps."

"I'm glad I'm not Bert," remarked Jay, "Seventy bumps!"

"Don't forget the one for luck," I said.

Jay laughed, "Oh God, yeah."

"You don't mean Lindon-on-Sea, do you?" asked Jason.

"That's it, yes, Lindon-on-Sea."

"Yeah, he likes that place. He used to bang on about it a lot, but he wasn't born there."

"No?"

"Nah," He took one last drag before he stubbed out the cigarette in an ashtray. "He was born in Tedford. Mum gave him up for adoption, and he was brought up mainly in children's homes. He only went to Lindon-on-Sea once on a trip with the home. Stayed at a B&B, Moon something or other. I can't remember. He went on about that for ages, too."

"A children's home? Never?"

"Yeah, true as I'm sitting here."

I felt a sudden spurt of compassion for Michael Lawrence until thoughts of his cruel, manipulating ways came to mind, and the bones, right there at the very forefront, bones that belonged to a lady called Elizabeth Marks, bones that had come into Michael Lawrence's possession somehow. Worst case scenario, that he'd murdered her and kept quiet about it for all this time, and then used her bones for a cruel prank. Thinking of all those things made my compassion for him disappear completely.

I drank the last of the Babycham as Jay said, "Right, let's get on to this, eh? If I can use your phone, Jack?" He looked at him questioningly, "I'll get Sergeant Hollis and Sergeant Crawford to take a trip out to Lindon-on-Sea as back-up. You and I can meet them out there, okay, Mandy? Are you up for that?"

I nodded, "Maybe we should visit Michael Lawrence's place first, though, Jay. Just in case he's turned up by now."

Jay drained his pint and stood up, "Yeah, okay. I'll go use the phone first." He disappeared behind the bar.

"It'll be like looking for a needle in a haystack?" said Jason, slowly shaking his head.

I shrugged, "It won't be easy, but as far as I can remember, Lindon-on-Sea is a fairly small place."

"Right," said Jay, "I spoke to Sergeant Crawford, and both are going to be heading out very soon. Come on, Mandy." We said goodbye to Jason as I waved at the gawping dog walkers and walked out of the pub.

CHAPTER FOURTEEN

Still September 1972 – Lindon-on-Sea

It was getting light as we arrived in Lindon-on-Sea, and we cruised past a sign with its thick black letters saying, *"Lindon-on-Sea Welcomes Careful Drivers."* The sun rose in an orange glow, the sky a dark line above it, and even from inside the car, the squawk of restless seagulls could be heard, along with the salty smell of the sea that hung in the air.

"I love the seaside, don't you?" I looked at Jay, at his profile, his straight nose and square chin, the dusky freckles on his skin, the little dimples when he smiled. I couldn't resist bursting into song, *"Oh I do like to be beside the seaside, oh I do like to be beside the sea…"*

I laughed, and Jay said, "You are extremely lively at such an early hour, Mandy."

"It's because we're at the seaside."

"I know, and yeah, I love it too. We used to go to the beach a lot, you know, before my parents died. It was great. Dad taught me to swim."

"You must have a lot of happy memories of them."

"I do, loads. I've a photo album at home with pictures of the three of us at the beach, the fun fair, and at the swimming pool. I'll show you sometime." He gave me a side-eyed smile and a wink before turning his gaze back to the road.

We cruised for a moment or two before Jay pulled over along the sea wall. It was quiet, so there were hardly any cars about; only a couple were parked, one of them being an unmarked police car with Sergeant Crawford and Sergeant Hollis inside. We got out of the car, and a strong sea breeze almost knocked us over as we made our way over to them. The sea was rough, huge waves heaving onto the smooth expanse of sand. Sergeant Crawford rolled down the car window, and Jay crouched down to speak with them.

"Morning, Sir."

"Hey, morning, Sergeant Crawford, Sergeant Hollis. Anything yet?"

"No, Sir, but now you two are here, we're going to split up and patrol both ends of the town. It's only a small place. We'll walkie-talkie you if we see anything."

"Okay. Anywhere around here we can get a decent bacon sandwich?"

"Yeah, we've just had one, haven't we?" He turned to Sergeant Hollis, who said, patting his stomach, "Yeah, delicious sandwich. A little café down the main street called *Betty's Baps.*

Jay grimaced, *"Betty's Baps,* eh? Great name."

"Yeah, nice little place, Sir, clean and all."

Jay stood up, "Oh, look out for a B&B called Moon something or other. Michael Lawrence stayed there once. You never know, he might go there, okay?"

"Yeah, definitely worth checking, Sir."

Jay and I set off then, walking across the road and onto the main street, which was full of shops that sold buckets and spades, huge towels featuring scenes of palm trees, the sea, and sand, sticks of striped rock, and swimming costumes for all shapes and sizes.

We soon found the café, Betty's Baps, and went inside;

a little bell on the door rang upon our arrival. It smelled of coffee, hot water, and fried food. Yet, it was snug and warm, and frilly curtains hung at the windows. It was quiet; just an older man alone with a cup of tea and a newspaper, and a woman with a small child, who nagged at the woman to hurry up and take her to the beach, *"It's too cold yet, darling,"* the mother said, *"Wait until it warms up a bit, oh, and for the tide to come in."*

The waitress told us to take a seat and she'd be with us in a jiffy. Music played from the jukebox, *"Sylvia's mother says Sylvia's busy, too busy to come to the phone..."*

"What are you having?" asked Jay, as he picked up the plastic menu and took a cursory glance. "Do you want coffee?"

"Yes, please, and a bacon sandwich. I can smell bacon, so it's got to be a bacon sandwich." *"Sylvia's mother says Sylvia's trying to start a new life of her own..."*

Jay laughed and sniffed the air like a bloodhound, nodding in agreement as the waitress came over, a notepad and pencil in her hand. I gazed in wonder at her hair, the tallest beehive I'd ever seen, heavily lacquered into place. She was wearing a pink and white striped overall, which reminded me of the sticks of rock we'd seen earlier in the shop. Quite fitting, really, for a beach setting.

"Please, Mrs. Avery, I just gotta talk to her, I'll only keep her awhile..."

"Do you think the waitress is Betty of Betty's baps?" I asked him.

Jay shook his head, "No, look at the lady behind the counter, the short, chubby one operating the coffee machine?" I nodded, "She's more likely to have the nickname of Betty's baps, don't you think?"

I giggled as I sipped at my coffee. It was thick and black, and the bacon crispy, the bread soft, and I knew I'd be coming back to this place, the name *"Betty's Baps,"* or not. "Wow, that was good, don't you think?"

"Mm, moreish," replied Jay, "Definitely moreish. I could do another round."

"There's just something about seaside places." *"Please, Mrs. Avery, I just want to tell her goodbye…"* "The fish and chips are always good too."

"Yeah. Hey, talking of seaside places, when all this is over, we should go on holiday somewhere." He picked up his mug of coffee and took a sip. I watched as he licked his lips with his tongue, my heart racing.

"What, here? You and me?" I said, still staring at him, unable to take my eyes away.

"What are you staring at, Mandy?"

"Me? Nothing. Nothing at all," I said, red-faced.

He grinned and winked, and my heart raced even more as, with a shrug, he said, "I didn't necessarily mean here. How about going abroad?"

"Abroad?" I almost choked on the last little bit of coffee, "Oh no, Jay, I don't think going abroad is for the likes of me."

"What are you talking about? People travel abroad frequently now. We could go to Spain. Majorca is supposed to be nice, warm, and sunny. How about that, eh?"

"I'd love to, but well, I can't imagine flying."

"I can see that, yeah, but look at how many people do fly. It can't be so bad, can it?"

"No, I suppose not, and it's something to think about, but first of all, we've got a criminal to catch, haven't we?"

"Yes, we have. It's just, well," He snaked his hand across the table and took hold of mine, "I can't wait for us to be alone together." He moved closer and lowered his voice, "With lots of time to, well, enjoy each other."

"Do you know," I whispered back, "I feel as if all my Christmases have come at once."

He squeezed my hand and gave me a soft kiss on the lips, and then smiled and said, "That's exactly how I feel, but as you say, we've work to do first. Come on, let's go and catch our criminal."

"Yes," I nodded. "It's about time Michael Lawrence paid for what he did."

***

Still September 1972 – Catching the Criminal

The walkie-talkie crackled into life and Sergeant Crawford's voice echoed eerily as Jay and I walked through the main shopping area in Lindon-on-Sea, "We found a B&B called *"Moonlighting,"* Sir. There isn't a Michael Lawrence staying there, but there is a Mick Leeson. Could be the same bloke. What do you think?"

"Yeah, could be. Is he there?"

"No, old fella on the reception said this Mick Leeson had breakfast in his room and then went off out about half an hour ago."

"Did you ask, maybe for a description of this Mick Leeson?"

"Yes, Sir, he said he's average height, dark hair, is wearing jeans and a blue walking jacket."

"Right, thanks for that, Sergeant, sounds very much like him, but you know jeans and walking jackets are popular things for people to wear. Look for any other B&Bs with a similar name; *"Moonlighting"* might not be the right place. We'll take a walk around the town and, if no joy there, then we'll head out onto the beach. Get Sergeant Hollis to stay by your car."

"Right you are, Sir."

The wind had picked up, blowing my hair all over my face, much to Jay's amusement as he watched me struggle to contain it beneath the hood of my coat. We conducted another check of the small town, but didn't see anybody matching that description, so we headed to the beach. Seagulls wheeled and cried, dive bombing into the sea, and riding the massive waves that threw up fish and crabs and strings of fleshy green seaweed onto the sands.

People walked with their dogs, muffled up to the eyeballs in their waterproof coats and woolly hats. I had a sudden longing for Sophie, the mean Chihuahua, or Bungle, the sweet little service dog, or indeed Max, my chubby lab, and Jessica, the border collie, as I watched our canine friends frolicking in the sea, getting soaked through and then shaking themselves dry all over their besotted owners. All my dogs would love this beach today.

The walkie-talkie crackled again, and Sergeant Hollis's agitated voice came through, "Sir, a man is walking the sands. He's wearing jeans and one of those walking jackets, blue it is."

"Um, yeah, that could be him. Whereabouts? Have you got a landmark?"

"Right in line with the children's funfair, Sir."

"Okay, we're heading that way. Keep him in sight, Sergeant Hollis."

"Right you are, Sir. Oh, I didn't mention, he's got a dog with him," The Sergeant's voice faded in and out with the wind, so we couldn't hear exactly what he said."

I frowned at Jay, "Did he say a dog?"

"A dog?" asked Jay.

"Yeah, a big white one," His voice suddenly came through loud and clear, "Wearing a bright blue harness."

"That's Wilson. Yes, it's him, Michael Lawrence. I wonder why the man at the B&B didn't mention the dog."

"Maybe Michael Lawrence isn't this Mick Leeson, and Michael Lawrence wasn't at the B&B at all."

"Yeah, makes sense."

The children's funfair came into view, its primary-colored rides bright against the backdrop of a grey sky flecked with filmy white clouds. Excited childish screams and shrieks echoed through the air. Jay took a pair of binoculars from his pocket and peered anxiously through them.

"You didn't tell me you had those?"

"I always carry them, you know, just in case." He gave me one of his mega-watt smiles, "They come in handy, especially in situations like this. Oh, and these." He pulled something from his coat pocket.

"Hand cuffs?"

"Yeah, hopefully I'll use them today." He handed me the binoculars, "Here, take a look. See if you can see our man."

"Wow, this is great. I can see every particle of sand and every drop of water in the sea."

Jay shook his head, "They're not that powerful, Mandy."

I giggled as I said, "They are Jay, a whale is coming right up onto the beach! Quick, let's go." I began to run as Jay said, "You idiot," and tried to wrestle the binoculars from me, but I held on tightly and peered through them again, "Oh Jay, I can see him, look…Michael Lawrence."

"I don't believe you. You're the boy who cried wolf."

"Boy?" I exclaimed.

"Okay, woman who cried wolf."

"It is him, look."

Grabbing the binoculars from me, he peered through, "Yep. It's him, alright. Come on."

We ran across the sands, our hearts beating fast, and yet, as if in a dream, Michael Lawrence and Wilson kept getting further and further away. I felt as if we weren't on the smooth sands at Lindon-on-Sea at all, but in a swamp and wading in quicksand, our steps labored and heavy.

"Stop, police," shouted Jay, but the words were immediately snatched from his mouth by the strong wind and thrown away into the atmosphere. I saw the pale oval of Michael Lawrence's face as he glanced over his shoulder, but he turned and kept running, his legs a blur propelling him further and further towards the sea. Yet Wilson stopped and, with a delighted bark, began to run towards us, his long legs carrying him quickly over the sands.

"Wilson," I said, "Hey Wilson." He began to jump up and down with excitement, his sandy paws on my coat, giving excited yips and yaps. Michael Lawrence stopped running and turned, his eyes darting all over the place as he searched for Wilson. When he saw Wilson with us, he seemed hesitant and unsure of what to do next.

"Oh my God," I said to Jay, "Wilson has rocks in a bag tied to his harness. Look," Untying them, I threw them onto the sand, "What was he planning to do?"

"Stay and hold onto Wilson," shouted Jay, "I'll get him."

He ran, and Sergeant Crawford and Sergeant Hollis puffed and panted in his wake. The wind roared and the sea threw itself up onto the shore, like a twin tub washer agitating laundry. People stopped and stared, their eyes wide, as Jay shouted, "Stop, Police," at the top of his voice, and grabbed Michael Lawrence's arm, bringing them both to a skid on the slippery sands, Sergeant Crawford and Sergeant Hollis close behind them.

"No, get off me. Leave me alone," screamed Michael Lawrence as he tried to pull away from Jay, but somehow, he kept hold of him. I could just about hear Jay's voice as he clipped the handcuffs onto Michael Lawrence's wrists, *"Michael Lawrence, I am arresting you on suspicion of the murder of Elizabeth Marks. You have the right to remain silent. Anything you say can and will be used against you in court. You have the right to a solicitor."*

"He's got rocks in his pockets, Sir," said Sergeant Crawford.

"What on earth were you going to do?" asked Jay.

Tears ran down his face, and he sniffed and snuffled, as he said, "No comment," and then, "Give me my dog." He turned around, shouting for Wilson, who, strained on the leash, trying to get closer to him.

"I'll take care of Wilson, Mick," I shouted over the wind, pulling hard on the lead to ensure Wilson stayed with me.

"We're taking you back to Lambuck Police Station, Mr. Lawrence," said Jay. He indicated to the two Sergeants, "Take him in the car with you two, okay? We'll take the dog."

"What about my car? It's in the car park behind the library."

"Don't worry about your car," said Sergeant Crawford, "Somebody will pick it up later. Here," He held out his hand, "Give me your keys."

I watched Sergeant Crawford take Michael Lawrence to the car and push his head down with a firm hand to help him into the back seat. Jay shook his head, "Looks like he was going to take the poor dog with him, doesn't it?"

I nodded, "Yeah, I'm happy we saved them. Oh God, what on earth is going to happen now?"

"Well, we wanted Michael Lawrence to pay for what he did, didn't we?"

I nodded as Jay said, "It looks like we're going to get our wish then, doesn't it?"

We got in the car, where Wilson lay regally in the back, and, as the engine coughed to life, Jay pulled smoothly away from the kerb, both of us relieved that we were on our way back to Lambuck and that, fingers crossed, we would soon find out what exactly had happened to Elizabeth Marks and who had done it.

CHAPTER FIFTEEN

4 October 1972 – Interview with Michael Lawrence

"Okay," said the Detective Inspector, as he switched on the tape recorder, "Today is Wednesday, 4 October 1972, Lambuck Police Station, Interview Room 2, and this is an interview with Mr. Michael Lawrence. The time is 12.00 pm. Present -Detective Inspector Jay Sutherland, Sergeant Leonard Hollis, and Sergeant Tony Crawford (Note Taker)."

Once again, I watched through the two-way mirror in Interview Room 1. Michael Lawrence looked pretty much the same, wearing blue jeans and a blue shirt. (Why was everything always blue with him? I mean, did he wear blue underwear and blue socks as well as blue jeans, a blue shirt, and a blue coat?) The song, "Song Sung Blue," kept coming into my mind every time I saw him, "Song sung blue, everybody knows one, song sung blue, every garden grows one..." Crazy, I know, but you can't help what goes through your head, can you?

Wilson had been living with me since Michael Lawrence's arrest. Jay had urged me to take him to the local dog rescue, "Doggy Days," but I was reluctant to do so, even though I was unsure if he and Herman would get along. However, they did (and still do) sleep, eat, and play together. I'm not sure if Herman will let me give Wilson back to Michael Lawrence now. Not without a fight, anyway.

Oh no, it's back again, "Song sung blue, weeping like a

willow, song sung blue, sleeping on my pillow…"

DI Jay Sutherland – *"You are entitled to legal representation, Mr. Lawrence."*

Mr. M Lawrence – *"I don't need it."*

DI Jay Sutherland – *"Mr. Lawrence, did you stay at the Moonlighting B&B in Lindon-on-Sea on the night of 23 September 1972?"*

Mr. M Lawrence – *"No, I did not. I slept in my car."*

DI Jay Sutherland – *"Why did you do that, Mr. Lawrence? Why sleep in your car when you could have the comfort of a B&B?"*

Mr. M Lawrence - *"I had my dog, Wilson, with me, and dogs aren't allowed in B&Bs. Well, not in that B&B anyway."*

DI Jay Sutherland – *"Have you stayed at the Moonlighting B&B before, Mr. Lawrence?"*

Mr. M Lawrence – *"Yeah, years ago when I was a kid."*

DI Jay Sutherland – *"With your parents?"*

Mr. M Lawrence – *"No, not exactly, um, no comment."*

DI Jay Sutherland – *"You don't want to answer that question?"*

Mr. M Lawrence – *"No. No comment."*

DI Jay Sutherland – *"Mr. Lawrence, please could you tell us here what you were planning on doing the day you were arrested at Lindon-on-Sea? Oh, and Mr. Lawrence, please bear in mind that the comment "no comment" won't cut it with this question."*

Mr. M Lawrence – *"What do you mean?"*

DI Jay Sutherland – *"You weighed your pockets down with rocks, Mr. Lawrence, and your dog, too. Bags of rocks were found tied to Wilson's harness."*

Mr. M Lawrence – *"Well, what do you think I was going to do? Have a nice little swim?"*

DI Jay Sutherland – *"Mr. Lawrence, we think you were*

going to walk into the sea with your dog, Wilson. You made that poor animal suffer. Now, why would you do that, Mr. Lawrence?"

Mr. M Lawrence – *"Because I guessed I was going to be arrested for murder when there's no way I would murder anyone, and I love my dog and want him with me. I didn't see the point anymore, you know."* He gazed from one police officer to the other. *"You've got the wrong man, but you wouldn't believe me if I told you who did it, would you?"*

DI Jay Sutherland – *"Who murdered Elizabeth Marks? If it wasn't you, Mr. Lawrence, then who did it?"*

Mr. M Lawrence – *(chuckling and grinning).*

DI Jay Sutherland – *"Who, Mr. Lawrence?"*

Mr. M Lawrence – *"Jason Rogan."*

A shiver ran through me at his words, and then anger that both Michael Lawrence and Jason Rogan were playing themselves off against each other. Each of them was accusing the other of being the murderer of Elizabeth Marks. One of them would have to come clean, surely?

DI Jay Sutherland – *(Frowning), "Jason Rogan? Are you sure, Mr. Lawrence?"*

Mr. M Lawrence – *"You see, I said you wouldn't believe me."*

DI Jay Sutherland – *"We need proof, Mr. Lawrence, evidence. Do you have any evidence?"*

Mr. M Lawrence – *"There is evidence, but I haven't got it. It's all at his house. Her belongings, and the belongings of others, too. I've seen it all. The cord he used."*

DI Jay Sutherland – *"The cord?"*

Mr. M Lawrence – *"The cord he used on Elizabeth Marks."*

DI Jay Sutherland – *"And the bones?"*

Mr. M Lawrence – *"He had all the bones stashed in his*

house. Okay, it was my idea to scare Mandy Morgan, to hide the bones with clues, but they were his bones. His souvenirs. Do you see what I mean?"

I felt sick, ill, and unsure, not knowing who to believe, torn between the two. They were both odd people, but, oh my God, we'd have to revisit Jason Rogan's house, scour it, and find the souvenirs that Michael Lawrence said he had hidden away. I found it hard to believe that Jason had done this, given that I had spoken to him on the night of the party. He said Michael Lawrence attacked him, but could it have been the other way around? I'm so confused.

DI Jay Sutherland – *"Who hid the bones, Mr. Lawrence?"*

Mr. M Lawrence – *"I did. It was tough, you know, thinking of different places, writing up the clues. Pretty clever really if you think about it."*

DI Jay Sutherland – *"Where does Mr. Rogan keep his souvenirs, Mr. Lawrence?"*

Mr. M Lawrence – *"In the cellar in a big old wooden box. A blanket box, I suppose you'd call it."*

DI Jay Sutherland – *"So, when Jason Rogan showed you the souvenirs, did you not think to tell the police?"*

Mr. M Lawrence – *"No, I wanted to use them, the bones that is, to scare Mandy Morgan. She thought she was better than me, superior, you know, and so did her friend, Steph, Stephanie Noble. I wanted to scare her, too, but well, you've caught me now, haven't you?"*

DI Jay Sutherland – *"Spoiled your fun, Mr. Lawrence?"*

Mr. M Lawrence – *"Yeah, spoiled my fun."* He sat back, a smirk on his face, arms crossed over his chest.

DI Jay Sutherland – *"Was it you, Mr. Lawrence, who used a cord to murder Elizabeth Marks?"*

Mr. M Lawrence – *"No, I didn't know the woman. It was Jason Rogan. Mandy Morgan was the girlfriend of Jason Rogan for a while, wasn't she?"*

DI Jay Sutherland – *"Miss Morgan isn't here to speak for herself, Mr. Lawrence, so no comment on that one."*

Mr. M Lawrence – *"Well, all I can say is, she's lucky to be alive."*

My heart, beating hard and fast, plummeted right down into my shoes.

DI Jay Sutherland – *"You didn't think to warn Miss Morgan about Jason Rogan?"*

Mr. M Lawrence – *"None of my business what she gets herself into, is it?"*

DI Jay Sutherland – *"Have you anything else to tell us, Mr. Lawrence?"*

Mr. M Lawrence – *"No, I have not."*

DI Jay Sutherland – *"Did you fight with Jason Rogan just before you set off to go to Lindon-on-Sea, Mr. Lawrence?"*

Mr. M Lawrence – *"Yeah, I did. He didn't want me to come clean. He wanted us both to go to Lindon-on-Sea and walk into the waves. He wanted to be gone, too, but I said no. I said he should stay in Lambuck and tell the police everything."*

DI Jay Sutherland – *"Thank you, Mr. Lawrence."*

The interview is over today, Wednesday, October 4, 1972, at 1:20 p.m. Thank you, everyone. He switched off the tape recorder with a click.

***

October 1972 – Tedford County Morgue

The morgue was cold, and there was a smell unlike any other. Something I couldn't put my finger on, something

I couldn't define, something that was part of the fabric of the room, something ingrained in the very walls.

I was with Jay, Sergeant Hollis, and the forensic team. I felt sick and shaky, probably because, unlike Jay and Sergeant Hollis, I'd never been in a morgue before. It's all very well finding bones individually, you can pretend they're not real, that they're plastic, that they're fake, but, seeing them in the shape of the person, all neatly mapped out, all the bones in their correct places, as they were when that person was alive and well, is a very different experience.

Jay nudged me with his elbow. "Are you okay, Mandy?"

I nodded and whispered, "Yeah," and then gave him a small smile, touched that he was worried about me, "I'll be okay."

"You, uh, look a little green around the gills," And then after a pause, "Fancy fish and chips later? Or" He shrugged, "A Chinese?"

"What?" A grin met my puzzled face, and then as the penny dropped, "I'll get you for this later, Jay," I whispered from the side of my mouth.

"Vesta beef curry?" he asked, his shoulders shaking with mirth.

The forensic expert, a Forensic Anthropologist as she was called, was a young lady named Millicent Fletcher. She wore bright red lipstick and had eyes as dark as sloes, but ashen skin. With a chill running down my spine, I wondered if her coloring had anything to do with the time she spent in the morgue, that maybe her skin was bleached by contact with the dead. Is that possible?

She looked a little like Morticia from the Addams

family? She had the same hairdo, long and black, and parted in the middle. Dear reader, I suspect you think I've gone crazy, and, do you know what, you could be right!

Trying to forget how sick I felt, I zoned in, to listen to what she said, "Hi everyone, thank you so much for coming here today to discuss the human bones that Detective Inspector Jay Sutherland has found (she nodded towards Jay) and Miss Mandy Morgan, a concerned member of the public (she inclined her head towards me). Oh, and by your dogs as well, Miss Morgan, is that right?" She leaned in close to me, all her large white teeth on display. "And in various places around the Lambuck area?"

Swallowing hard, I said, "Yes, I'm a dog walker and, well, we followed clues leading us to the different bones which, yes, have been found in different places around Lambuck. It's been, um, interesting to say the least." I giggled and, guess what? Millicent Fletcher giggled right back. Good for her, eh?

"Thank you, Miss Morgan. Now, from the bones we have found out that they belong to a young woman, she was 28 years old at death, and her name was Elizabeth Louise Marks. She was Caucasian and stood at 5 feet 7 inches. From the cold case, we know she went missing just over eight years ago in September 1964. The last sighting of her was by her parents on 16 September 1964. She called in to see them before meeting a friend. Unfortunately, she didn't tell them where she was going or with whom she was going. All the bones are present, except for two finger digits and one toe digit. So, 203 bones out of 206 isn't bad, eh?

"The one important thing we have seen is a depression in the skull, a slight hair line fracture," She picked up the skull to show us what she meant, pointing it out with a red painted finger nail, "This indicates trauma and could well be the cause of death, the skull having been hit from above with a heavy object."

The small hole in the skull came back to me then. I remembered seeing it when I'd found it, and the thin black line running from the hole. Of course, it had to be that a heavy object had hit her to cause that. I thought then of the cord that Michael Lawrence had mentioned, insinuating, or wanting us to believe, that Jason Rogan had strangled Elizabeth Marks. I had to ask a question to clarify this. My heart beating fast, I raised my hand.

"Miss Morgan?" Millicent Fletcher raised her eyebrows. "How may I help?"

"Is there any indication the victim was strangled?"

She shook her head, "There are no fractures to the hyoid bone, which is the bone at the top of the neck, and there's no pinpoint hemorrhages either. So, no, death wasn't caused by strangulation."

Jay and I exchanged a glance, no doubt thinking the same thing, that Michael Lawrence had lied to us about there being a cord at Jason Rogan's house. We needed to search his place as soon as possible.

"Thank you for this, Miss Fletcher," said Jay, "You've been very helpful."

"Yes, thank you," I repeated as we all shook hands, and Jay and I left the morgue. Outside, I took great deep breaths of air, gulping and gulping as if I couldn't get enough of it, as if I'd been starved of far nicer smells like car exhaust fumes and rotten eggs for years and years.

"If the skull was hit from above with a heavy object, that's murder, isn't it?"

Jay nodded, "It's all pointing to it, yeah."

"Right," said Jay, "A thorough search of Jason Rogan's place first to see if we can find any weapon at all, oh, and to get the box in the cellar, and then we get him in. Okay?"

I nodded as Jay carried on, "Quite an experience that, eh, Mandy?"

"Yeah, I don't know why it made me feel so sick. After all, there were only bones, no blood or body organs or anything like that. It was just seeing all the bones together, the full person."

"Yeah, I know what you mean, and, as well as that, the first time in the morgue is always a bit traumatic. It's that sweetish smell. It takes ages to get rid of it. It seems to cling on, if you know what I mean?"

"Yeah, you're right there."

"Sure, you don't fancy a curry?"

"Oh you," I growled at him, just like Sophie the mean Chihuahua, while he laughed, deep, gut-wrenching laughter. "Go on," I said, "Go. Or I'll hit you with my handbag. Vesta Beef curry indeed!"

"Help," Jay said, as he raced away, "Help!"

"You just wait until I get hold of you."

He held out his arms, and I ran into their safe curve, "Ooh, I can't wait for that!"

***

October 1972 – Voicemail from Mum

"Mandy? It's Mum. Are you there? Look, I'll leave you a message if you're not there. I'm off to see your dad. I've come to my senses, love, and I just wanted to say that, well, I'm sorry for putting all that stuff on you, about your dad having an affair. Your dad wouldn't do that, no way. And all that stuff about lipstick on his shirt. I'm sorry, I really am, but well, I really believed it at the time.

"Anyway, I thought you'd be glad to know I've joined the Real Ale Club at the *Rabbit and Bear*. I've been a couple of times and it's great, better than sitting home on my own smoking and worrying that your dad has another woman. I get dressed up too, so your dad can see what he'd be missing if he left me at home. You know, nice outfit, bit of red lippy. Secretly, though, I think he's glad I go with him now. He only said the other day, "It's a lot better than you nagging at me, Angela."

"Bert and Rosemary (who I thought was a scarlet woman) are members too, and oh my, what fun we have with them, such a lovely couple. We might be going on holiday with them next year. Not just your average Butlins here in the UK, but abroad, perhaps. What do you think of that? I bet you never thought that Dad and I would get on an airplane, did you? Not one of them flying machines, eh?

"You must come along some time with Jay, you know, to the Real Ale Club. He's nice, isn't he (nudge, nudge, wink wink), you lucky thing, Mandy. Oh, and he's so generous, too. Having a box of real ales delivered to your dad every month for a year, just so he could dig in the allotment, is far beyond what was expected of him. I'd have let him dig for nothing but, you know, your dad, he's always been a bit of a tightwad.

"Anyway, gotta go, he's shouting for me. In a hurry, he is, for his pint of real ale. Oh, I think he's retired from his job as one of the ciggy police, because he not only doesn't have a moan when I smoke but even lights them up for me. Carries a lighter everywhere with him now. True gentleman. See you soon, Mandy. Hopefully, in the *Rabbit and Bear,* along with your Detective Inspector. Love ya!"

CHAPTER SIXTEEN

10 October 1972 – Interview with Jason Rogan

"Okay," said the Detective Inspector, as he switched on the tape recorder, "Today is Tuesday, 10 October 1972, Lambuck Police Station, Interview Room 2, and this is an interview with Mr. Jason Rogan. The time is 9.30 am. Present -, Detective Inspector Jay Sutherland, Sergeant Leonard Hollis, and Sergeant Tony Crawford (Note Taker)."

Once again, I'm watching this interview in the two-way mirror in interview room 1, and I'm very interested in what Jason Rogan has to say. The large blanket box retrieved from Jason Rogan's cellar was here now, on the floor beside the table where Jason Rogan was sitting. I noticed he glanced nervously at it from time to time, although he knew it would be here. After all, he was at his home when the police took it away. It would be more than interesting to see what's inside, and, hopefully, this interview would clear up any misunderstandings about what happened to Elizabeth Marks.

Just for the record, the contents of the box are now being displayed by Sergeant Hollis as follows: -

Exhibit 3 – One Ingersoll watch with engraving on the back *"with love to our dear daughter, Elizabeth, on your 18th, from Mum & Dad."*

Exhibit 4 – One pair of marcasite earrings, heart-shaped.

Exhibit 5 – One ring, a thin gold band.

Exhibit 5 – One pair of gingham check capri pants.

Exhibit 6 – One short-sleeved white blouse.

Exhibit 7 – One suede fringed jacket.

I felt so sad to see the clothes that Elizabeth Marks wore before her death.

The box was now empty, and there was no cord.

DI Jay Sutherland – *"You are entitled to legal representation, Mr. Rogan.*

Mr. J Rogan – *"I don't need it."*

DI Jay Sutherland – *"Mr. Rogan, where were you on the evening of 16 September 1964?"*

Mr. J Rogan – *"You having me on or what?"*

DI Jay Sutherland – *"No, Mr. Rogan, I can assure you I'm not having you on. It's a reasonable question, and I require an answer.*

Mr. J Rogan – *"It's years ago, man. I was only 19 years old."*

DI Jay Sutherland – *"Yeah, but don't they say you remember your teenage years more than any other?"*

Mr. J Rogan – *"I can't remember."*

DI Jay Sutherland – *"Well, let me jog your memory a little, eh? Did you have a date with a lady called Elizabeth Marks that evening?"*

There was a long, painful silence during which Jason Rogan stared into space, his face a white, paper-like mask.

DI Jay Sutherland – *"Mr. Rogan, please answer my question. Whatever happened that night will eventually come to light. You must have known that when you allowed Michael Lawrence to bury the bones of the deceased woman for a prank.*

Mr. J Rogan – *"I just knew that man would be my undoing. I told him not to do it, but would he listen? No! He just never does.*

We'll never get found out, he said, nobody will ever know."

DI Jay Sutherland – *"Explain yourself, Mr. Rogan."*

Mr. J Rogan – *"Okay, yeah, I had a date that evening with Elizabeth Marks."*

The atmosphere in the room became electric, like every light had been put on at full wattage, a glaring bright white, and Detective Inspector Jay Sutherland and Sergeant Hollis all leaned forward, their elbows on the table, and Sergeant Crawford had his pencil poised and at the ready, as if they were going to lap up every word Jason Rogan spoke.

Mr. J Rogan – *"I liked her, Elizabeth Marks. She was pretty and fun, and I'd been wanting to go out with her for what seemed like forever. I asked her many times, and on this day, she finally agreed to meet me at the Rabbit and Bear pub at 8:00 pm.*

"Well, I did, and we had a great time. We just had a couple of drinks, and then I asked her if she wanted to come back to my place. Not the place I live in now, I had a flat then on Anchorage Grove, just around the back of Lambuck Library, near the Freestone building, you know where I mean? I'd only just left home then and was getting the place together. I was proud of it and proud to invite her round."

DI Jay Sutherland – *"Yeah, we know where you mean. What happened, Mr. Rogan?"*

Mr. J Rogan – *"She didn't seem too sure at first about coming back to my place but then asked me if I had a color TV. I said I had, not everybody did in those days, but I worked in a TV repair shop in Tedford at that time, my first job since college, and I got a cheap deal renting a cool set. She was excited; she wanted to watch Peyton Place, she said, her favorite program in the world. She was in love with Ryan O'Neal. So, she said she would come back to my place if she could watch the TV, and of course I said yes."*

DI Jay Sutherland – *"Okay, carry on, Mr. Rogan."*

Mr. J Rogan – *"Well, we had another couple of drinks at my place, just a couple of shots of whisky from a bottle I filched from my mum and dad's place when I left. I had the remains of a fire in the fireplace still smoldering, so I stoked it up a bit. Then we sat on the settee together and exchanged a couple of kisses, when she broke away and reminded me about the TV, so I switched it on. But there was nothing - no picture, no sound; the damn thing just wasn't working.*

"I tried all sorts to get it working, looked at the plug, the aerial, oh man, I tried so hard to get that TV working but with no luck and she was having a go at me, picking and piking, and saying I did it on purpose to get her round there and that she thought I had bad intentions towards her. I told her I didn't have bad intentions, that I liked her and wanted us to go out together.

"Well, as soon as I said that she jumped up from the settee and said she had to go. She said it had been a mistake to go out with me that night, and she didn't want to see me ever again. I asked her why. What had I done wrong? Was it because of the TV? And she said no, it wasn't that, but she was going. I grabbed her arm, but she pulled away, heading for the door, and, oh God, the times I've thought of this and wished I'd let her go straight out of that door, but I didn't."

DI Jay Sutherland – *"Carry on, Mr. Rogan."*

Mr. J Rogan – *"I got mad because she was going. She'd only come back with me because of the TV, so I was hurt, you know, I liked her. So, I grabbed her arm again, and she lashed out, and her nails scratched my face, and drew blood. It hurt you know, so I pushed her, and she staggered backwards, falling and hitting her head on the coffee table. And, well, that's it, that's what happened."*

DI Jay Sutherland – *"And that was it? Elizabeth Marks*

died because she hit her head on your coffee table?"

Mr. J Rogan *(nodding his head) – "Yeah, that's what happened. I went to her straight away, knelt beside her, and there was blood pooling around her head. I shook her, I felt for the pulse in her neck, but there wasn't one."*

Jason Rogan began to cry, great gulping sobs, sitting with his elbows on his thighs, his head hanging. Detective Inspector Jay Sutherland pushed a box of tissues over the table.

DI Jay Sutherland *– "So what did you do then? Why didn't you call an ambulance?"*

Mr. J Rogan *– "I didn't call an ambulance, man, because I was scared. How could I explain what had happened, without it looking bad on me? After all, I pushed her. They'd have had me banged up for murder."*

DI Jay Sutherland *– "You could have told the truth. After all, people had seen you together in the Rabbit and Bear, hadn't they?"*

Mr. J Rogan *– "No, it was strange that night in there. Jack, the landlord, was away on holiday, and I didn't know anyone else to contact. All strangers that night, including the temporary landlord. Not a single familiar face."*

DI Jay Sutherland *– "Okay, so what did you do next?"*

A long silence, just sniffing and crying, pulling tissue after tissue from the box.

Mr. J Rogan *– "I rang Michael Lawrence. Okay, he wasn't a mate exactly, being as he was like ten years older than me, but we talked sometimes in the pub, and he came round to my place straight away, and got rid of the body. Told me not to ask any questions and he'd tell no lies."*

DI Jay Sutherland *– "Why him, why Michael Lawrence? Just because you talked in the pub?"*

Mr. J Rogan – *"No. I don't know. I just felt I could trust him, and that he knew his way around things like that."*

DI Jay Sutherland – *"Things like what?"*

Mr. J Rogan – (shrugging) *"Things that are against the law."*

DI Jay Sutherland – *"Did he seem surprised, shocked, anything at all when he saw Elizabeth Marks dead on your sitting room floor? Did he suggest phoning the police or an ambulance?"*

Mr. J Rogan – *"No, like I say, I think he was always dabbling in breaking with the law."*

DI Jay Sutherland – *"Michael Lawrence said you keep your souvenirs in this box here, Mr. Rogan?"*

Mr. J Rogan – *"I think they're more his souvenirs than mine. He put them there."*

DI Jay Sutherland – *"Please look at exhibits 3 to 7 on display here, Mr. Rogan. Was Elizabeth Marks wearing this outfit on the evening she died?"*

Mr. J Rogan – *"Yes, I believe she was wearing that, or something similar at least."*

DI Jay Sutherland – *"So, you didn't know what Michael Lawrence did with the body of Elizabeth Marks?"*

Mr. J Rogan – *"No, I didn't. When I got back, it was gone, and all the mess was cleaned up too."*

DI Jay Sutherland – *"Back from where?"*

Mr. J Rogan – *"He told me to make myself scarce while he did what he had to do. I just walked around the streets, my head was over all the place, man, and I can't tell you how relieved I was when I got back, and she was gone. I could sort of pretend it had never happened and, well, that's what I think I've done for all these years."*

DI Jay Sutherland – *"Mr. Rogan, Mr. Lawrence told us there was a cord in the box in your cellar that you used on Elizabeth*

Marks."

Mr. J Rogan – "What?"

DI Jay Sutherland – "Mr. Lawrence insinuated that you strangled Elizabeth Marks with a cord which you kept in your box of souvenirs. Is this true or false?"

Mr. J Rogan – His whole demeanor angry, his eyes flashing, rising from his chair, "Why, it's false. I've just told you the truth about what happened. And did you find a cord in that box?"

DI Jay Sutherand – "Sit down, Mr. Rogan. No. There was no cord."

Mr. Rogan reluctantly sat down – a silence.

DI Jay Sutherland – "Have you anything else to tell us, Mr. Rogan?"

Mr. J Rogan – "No, I don't think so. I have a question, though."

DI Jay Sutherland – "Go ahead."

Mr. J Rogan – "What will happen to me now?"

DI Jay Sutherland – "That's for the court to decide, Mr. Rogan, both for you and Mr. Lawrence. Anything else?"

Mr. J Rogan – "No. But I want to say, for the record, that I didn't mean to hurt Elizabeth Marks. I liked her and, well, what happened, it's been giving me nightmares for years and…well, that's all."

DI Jay Sutherland – "Thank you, Mr. Rogan, but well, the thing is the injury sustained by Elizabeth Marks as the cause of death was a heavy instrument hitting her head from above, and not consistent at all with hitting her head on your coffee table. What do you say to that, Mr. Rogan?"

Mr. J Rogan – Giggling nervously. "What are you talking about? That's what happened. She fell and hit her head on the coffee table. And that's the truth."

DI Jay Sutherland – *"Have you got a coffee table, Mr. Rogan?"*

Mr. J Rogan – *"Um, no, not now. I got rid of it after what happened. Couldn't bear to look at it, you know, so, um, took it to a charity shop."*

DI Jay Sutherland – *"And which charity shop was that, Mr. Rogan?"*

Mr. J Rogan – *"Oh, the one next door to the baker's in Lambuck."*

DI Jay Sutherland – *"Right, thank you, Mr. Rogan."*

The interview is over today, Tuesday, October 10, 1972, at 11:00 a.m. Thank you, everyone. He switched off the tape recorder with a click.

***

10 October 1072 – *The evening of the day of the Interview in the Rabbit and Bear*

"I'm, I'm so in love with you, whatever you want to do, is all right with me…"

"Oh my God, who do you believe?" I asked Jay.

We were in the *Rabbit and Bear*, sitting at the bar on high stools that had legs long and slim as dancers. The place was quiet; just a few after-work drinkers stood around the bar, while others sat at tables, treating themselves to chicken and chips for a late supper. He shrugged and took a sip of his pint, "Well, Jason Rogan must be lying. Do you remember if he had a coffee table or not?"

"He didn't have one when I knew him, but it could be true that he got rid of it. We could check with the charity shop. I don't think the shop in Lambuck takes furniture. Well, they don't now."

"But if it was a blow from above to the skull?"

"Then she couldn't have knocked it on the coffee table, could she?"

"He was wrong to get Michael Lawrence involved, wasn't he?" I drank a little of the Babycham, the bubbles popping up my nose, "That was his biggest downfall. If Michael Lawrence hadn't used the bones as he did, none of this would have come to light. Elizabeth Marks would still be one of the many missing girls."

"Well, he's done her a favor then, at least she can be laid to rest at long last." Sadly, Jay shook his head, "The future doesn't look good for either of them, I'm afraid." *"Ooh baby, let's, let's stay together (Together), loving you whether, whether times are good or bad, happy or sad…"*

"We need to find the murder weapon, don't we?"

"Yeah, we do, but I can't imagine that it would have been disposed of in the local area as the bones were. Can you?"

I shook my head, "No, probably not. You know what, though, I can't believe I've been out with both of those weirdos. I do have a poor choice in men, don't I? Jason Rogan could well be a murderer, and Michael Lawrence gets rid of dead bodies without a second thought."

"Yeah, you're right there, but really? A poor taste in men. I think maybe your current boyfriend is okay."

"I didn't mean you, Jay," Leaning towards him, I planted a soft kiss on his lips, sending shivers racing through my body, "You're the best." And then suddenly Mum's voicemail came to mind, and I said, "I have a bone to pick with you, though! Oh, and excuse the pun."

"Hey, a pun, eh? Clever…" The mega-watt smile left

his face at the look I gave him, "What?"

"Did my dad blackmail you so we could dig in his allotment?"

"Ah, the real ale?"

I nodded, "A full case every month? That is so…"

"We had to dig in the allotment, and if that was the only way, then so be it," He smiled wryly, "It had to be done, Mandy."

"You just wait until I speak to my dad."

"No, don't say anything. Please. How did you find out, anyway?"

"My mum thought I knew and mentioned it in her voicemail. Honestly, I thought better of Dad."

"Your dad's alright. He's offered to share the beer with me anyway. *"Let's, let's stay together, loving you whether, whether times are good or bad, happy or sad…"* "And, well, if he ever gets to be my father-in-law, I'd consider myself lucky."

"Father-in-law? Why Jay…" In shock, my hands shaking and my heart racing, I downed the rest of the Babycham.

"Yeah," and then almost shyly, his face a burning red, "Marry me?"

"Are you serious?"

"Of course, I am. Will you?"

"Yes, oh yes, I will," I replied, as the thought, "Wow, how come men that look like Greek Gods are suddenly available for me, Mandy Morgan?"

"I meant it when I said I loved you, but you know that, don't you?"

"Yeah, do you know what? I think you do, and I love you too."

CHAPTER SEVENTEEN

November 1972

"It's just a quick meeting," said Steph, "I've got to get back to work and I'll get…"

"Yeah, I know you'll get killed if you're late…" She bit into her sandwich and munched hungrily.

"Don't mock me, Mandy, it's true."

"I've got to get back too. Sophie, the mean Chihuahua, will be waiting for me."

"Yeah, with crossed legs," quipped Steph. We giggled like small children.

We're in our favorite place, Woolworths Café, and it was busy as usual, with all the tables full, so we were having to stand at a little ledge, a sort of makeshift table that juts out from the wall.

"Mm, this coffee is great," commented Steph. She took a deep draft, "The best coffee in the world." The din of voices was loud with people talking and laughing, and background music played, but because of the noise, I couldn't hear what it was.

I bit into my sandwich, tangy cheddar and Branston pickle exploded in my mouth, "Um, lovely sandwich." I munched leisurely, eyes closed as if I was in Heaven, and then, "Good old Woollies, eh, Steph? The best food and coffee, ever. Now, what did you want to see me about?"

"I just wanted to give you this." She held up a necklace,

a piece of black leather with what appeared to be a white bone hanging from it.

Gingerly, I took it from her. "What is it?" I grimaced, "And why give it to me?"

She shrugged, "Mick gave it to me. It's a tribal bone, apparently, a tooth or something, and I thought you might know what to do with it. I can't bear to wear it now. Not after everything that's happened."

I brought it closer and gazed at it, my eyes narrowed, "A tribal bone? I don't think so, and it doesn't look like a tooth; it appears more like a digit to me. A finger," And then an awful thought occurred to me, "Oh my God, Steph." The coffee machine whooshed steam into the air, which mingled with the cigarette smoke that hung in great balloons above our heads.

"What?"

"So, Michael Lawrence gave you this?"

"Yeah, he did. He said it was extraordinary and that I should wear it as protection."

"Protection? He told you some tall stories, didn't he? Didn't you see it looked more like a finger than a tooth?"

"No, not really, I just believed what he said, but now I know what an idiot he is, it doesn't surprise me that he lied about it being a tribal bone."

I lowered my voice and leaned in close to her, "I think it's one of Elizabeth Marks' missing fingers. According to Millicent Fletcher, she's a Forensic Anthropologist by the way, there are two fingers and one toe missing, or maybe just one finger and one toe now."

"Ugh," she said, disgusted, "And I've been wearing that around my neck?"

I nodded as she said, "All this stuff is creeping me out."
"Yeah, me too."
"What's happening with those two, anyway? Have they put them away yet?"
"They're in custody. The case won't go to trial for at least two or three months, but at least they're being kept inside, away from people. No bail either, which is great."
Carefully, I put the necklace into my rucksack. "I'll take it to Jay. The Forensics team will be able to determine if it belongs to Elizabeth Marks, but based on what has happened so far, the evidence points strongly to that conclusion. Why else would Michael Lawrence give it to you, if not to get at me?"
She checked her watch, "I've got to go, Mandy. Hey, maybe we can meet up in the *Rabbit and Bear* one night. When you get over your obsession with your gorgeous Detective Inspector, that is." She giggled as she put the strap of her bag over her head, wrapping it crosswise around her body.
"Hmm," I said, smiling, "My obsession isn't going to go away any time soon." I picked up my bags and followed her as we went out onto the street. It was a beautiful October day, and the sun shone in a blue sky. Leaves, their colors of orange and red, were breathtakingly beautiful, as they spun through the air.
She gave me the side-eye and a nudge with her elbow, "What does that mean?"
"Well," I felt stupid now, embarrassed almost. Steph and I had always said we'd never let a man come too close to our friendship, but at that time, I hadn't met the love of my life. I blurted it out, "He's asked me to marry him."
"Oh wow, oh Mandy," She flung her arms around me,

"Can I be your bridesmaid?"

"Yes, definitely yes, I can't think of anyone better for the job than you."

"Cool, look, I've got to dash, I'll get killed if I'm late for work. See ya."

I watched her go, tottering on her platform heels, her long brown hair swinging yet still with the obsession that she was going to be killed by the Providential Building Society. Did she know something I didn't? Was there some plot?

I shrugged, "Oh, well, as if there wasn't enough going on in my life now, and I still had a hunch about something. A silly hunch, perhaps, but I wasn't sure if Jason Rogan had ever had a coffee table in his flat. I'd never seen one, and I'd visited him a few times. Maybe he'd got rid of it, after what happened to Elizabeth Marks, but I wasn't convinced he'd ever had one at all.

***

October 1972 – Another Find in the Park

The dog walkers were standing in their usual scrum and turned to look at me as I walked through the park with Sophie the mean Chihuahua and, of course, Wilson, the large white poodle, who I think of as my dog now, and who lives harmoniously with me and my kitty cat, Herman.

"Adopted him, have you? Wilson, I mean," asked Lydia, her face back to its usual pallor after the clown make-up she wore when I saw her at Bert's 70th birthday party.

I shrugged, "I don't know for sure. Mick might want him back if he gets out."

"He won't get out, will he?" sneered John the wiry pensioner, "God help us all if he does. We don't want one such as him walking dogs with us, do we?" Sophie, the mean Chihuahua, began to growl very deep in her throat as Charlotte, Lydia's dog, began, very unwisely, to edge nearer to her in a friendly manner.

"No, we certainly don't," chimed in Liz, the dumpy woman with a cap of grey hair-tinged a fashionable pink, "His reputation's shot, and we'd run him out of town anyway."

"Where do you think we are?" I asked her, "The wild west? Are we heading for a shootout?" I giggled, but their faces were blank, all of them blank-faced at my little quip. Oh, for fellow dog walkers with a sense of humor, eh?

"Oh well," I said, "I'm off then. See you later." Charlotte, really trying her luck, edged even closer, but with a menacing snap from Sophie, the mean Chihuahua, she turned and ran, her tail firmly between her legs.

Off we went, Sophie, Wilson, and I, as far away from the other dog walkers as we could. I let Wilson off the leash, and he went straight into the bushes where he lifted his leg and then squatted, after which he was quiet, just a faint whining from amongst the leaves. With a feeling of apprehension, I remembered Max acting the same way when he found the skull, a plaintive whine, then in for the kill. I fed Sophie treats that she gobbled up quickly.

"Wilson?" I peered into the bushes, shaking the bag of treats for good measure, "Wilson?" No response. I gave one final, deafening shout," Wilson! " which did the trick, as he bounded out, his long legs a blur, and happily deposited something at my feet. Then, he looked up at me, a big smile on his face.

All I could think was, "Oh no, not another bone? Don't tell me it's all starting again." It wasn't, though, a bone, I mean, but maybe something equally important, for it was a long, thin poker, a fire poker, covered in dirt and remnants of ash, and splattered with rusty-looking marks, marks that looked like, oh good God, was it blood? Could this be it, the murder weapon? I remembered Jason Rogan's words, "*I had the remains of a fire in the fireplace still smoldering, so I stoked it up a bit.*" A shiver ran down my spine.

Gingerly, I picked it up, glad I was wearing gloves and, after a closer inspection, deposited it into my rucksack. I carried on with my walk, my mind whirring with sinister thoughts, all featuring the absence of a coffee table and now what looked like a blood-stained poker. I needed to speak with Jay, so once I'd taken Sophie the mean Chihuahua and Wilson home, I'd make my way to Lambuck police station to see Detective Inspector Jay Sutherland and tell him, oh, not what I'd found, but what Wilson had found.

***

December 1972 – Majorca

"*Oh, I do like to be beside the seaside, oh I do like to be beside the sea…*"

I glanced at Jay lying on the sand right next to me, looking like nothing but a Greek God. My gaze roamed up and down his body, from his floppy blonde hair to his broad chest flecked with light-colored hairs, tapering down to a slim waist, and then lower still to his black hip-hugger swimming trunks, and lower still to his long, slender legs. Oh my, my heart was beating so hard, I could die.

"What are you looking at, Mandy?"

"*Oh! I do like to stroll along the Prom, Prom, Prom! Where the brass bands play, "tiddly-om-pompom!"*"

"Me? Why, nothing, except the sea and the sand, and the clouds, although there's only one or two. Nothing to worry about. None of them dark, there's no rain forecast."

"Not like there will be at home, eh?"

"This place is not like home. This place is a paradise." I took a deep breath, inhaling the scent of salt and sun oil. Seagulls squawked and flew overhead like great white doves.

Jay sat up and looked around. "Yep, aquamarine sea, golden sand, hot sun, what more could we want??"

"There's hardly anybody around, either. Look, just a few children over there playing with buckets and spades," I pointed with a finger. "A couple of people over there. We've virtually got the whole beach to ourselves."

Jay nodded, "Yeah, it's great."

"Do you know something? I never thought somebody like me would ever be able to come to a place like this."

"What do you mean, somebody like you?"

"Oh, I don't know, somebody ordinary, with just an ordinary job and an ordinary house."

Jay laughed, "There's nothing ordinary about you, Mandy. You're one of the most interesting people I've ever met."

"What? Are you kidding?"

"No, I'm not, you're enthusiastic and it's catching. It certainly makes me happy. And anyway, this is just the start of it, the start of travel. People will soon be flying to all those far-flung places that previous generations would have never dreamed of visiting. Technology will boom and computers will become more and more important, maybe even phones, people carrying phones, you know."

"Are you crazy? Computers are good, yeah, but

they're huge. Typewriters with a carry case are the way to go. And phones? Why would anyone want to carry a phone around with them? There's no need, and anyway, it would be cumbersome." I gazed at him, at his strong profile, as I sifted sand, so smooth and silky, through my fingers.

"Yeah, okay," He gave me a sideways smile, "I could be wrong."

There was a comfortable silence with only the shushing of the sea and plaintive cries of seagulls filling the air. A couple came onto the beach and proceeded to lay down towels on the sands, a cool box nearby, from which they produced bottles of beer, as they sat idly looking out to sea. Someone switched on a radio, and music sounded: *"Song sung blue, everybody knows one..."* reminding me straight away of Michael Lawrence and his inevitable blue clothes.

I looked at Jay. "Are you glad it's all over?"

"You mean, glad that we cracked the case?"

I nodded, "Oh yes. The most important thing is that I'm glad the family of Elizabeth Marks finally has closure on what happened to her. Closure to grieve properly."

"Yes, you're right, that's the best part. I thought the funeral service was lovely, didn't you?"

"Yeah, it was, and her family seems like good people."

"Yeah, not like Jason Rogan and Michael Lawrence. I can't believe I went out with Jason for four months and never once suspected he was a dangerous person. I was slightly more suspicious of Michael Lawrence for some reason."

"Hmm, well, maybe you never found anything about Jason as odd because he killed Elizabeth Marks in a fit of rage, sort of like a rejection rage. You accepted him, did you?" He turned towards me, "If you hadn't, you might have seen that side of him."

"No, he rejected me," I told him, "And do you know, I don't know who she was," I shrugged, "I suppose I didn't care, even then."

He shook his head, "He must have been mad to finish with you, but then again, if he hadn't, you might not be here with me now." He nodded knowingly, "He did me a favor."

"Oh, I don't know," I said with a giggle, "I think I'd have noticed you at some point, Jay."

He reached out a hand to grasp mine, and pulled me closer and then closer still, until our lips touched, light as a feather, his so warm and salty. He broke away and gazed into my eyes, and then increased the pressure of his lips on mine until I felt as if I was melting into the sand, luxuriating in the heat of his touch.

"Shall we have a drink?" he asked, his lips soft against my neck.

"Yes, the champagne?"

I pulled the bottle from our beach bag, and Jay expertly popped the cork. He poured two glasses; the champagne frothed over the top, running sweet and sticky down his hand and disappearing into the sand.

"Hmm, you seem expert at that, have you opened a bottle before?"

Jay shook his head, "Not for something as important as this." He gave me a sexy wink.

I took a tentative sip. "Wow, I'm surprised, it's so similar to Babycham." The bubbles popped up my nose, and I giggled.

"Yeah, but far more expensive," He grinned and then said, "To us." He raised his glass high, "To a long and happy marriage, eh, Mrs. Sutherland?"

"Yes, Mr. Sutherland, to a long and happy marriage."

We clinked glasses and drank together, and then kissed again, his lips sticky from the champagne. I sipped the bubbly drink and held out my glass for more. Jay filled it up, and the liquid bubbled up and spilled over onto my hand.

"The poker was a magnificent find," Jay said, "Clinched the whole thing. I still can't believe Wilson found it in the park. Wouldn't you think the two of them would have hidden it better than that?"

"Hmm, I think they wanted everything to be found, wanted everything to come to an end. Look what Michael Lawrence wanted to do at Linton-on-Sands. Even though Jason Rogan used the poker, neither of them could live with the guilt of killing Elizabeth Marks, Michael Lawrence, particularly."

"Yep, you could be right."

"And it also helped to know that there never was a coffee table, didn't it?"

"Yeah, you were right about that too, and that the charity shop didn't take furniture, even back then in 1964. Everything coming together like that was so sweet, Mandy."

"Yep, we cracked it, with a little help from our friends, of course." I counted off on my fingers, "Sophie the mean Chihuahua, Bungle the service dog, Max the chubby lab, Jessica the border collie, Wilson, of course, and Bella, the lab. Oh, and talking of Wilson, with Michael Lawrence in custody, he won't come looking for my dog anytime soon.

Jay shook his head, "I don't think you could give him up anyway, could you?"

I shook my head, "No way, and Herman won't either,

nor my mum and dad. They dote on him."

"Yeah," He said with a side-eyed wink, "But only until they get a few grandchildren, don't you think?"

"A few? How many children do you want, Jay?"

He shrugged, "I'm not sure, four? Six?"

"Oh my God, that many. I'd be happy with two"

"Well, in that case, so would I." Leaning forward, Jay kissed my bare shoulder, his lips warm and dry.

"Our wedding day was fabulous, don't you think?"

"The best day of my life, Mandy."

"Truly?"

"Truly."

"Steph, my beautiful bridesmaid, seemed to spend a lot of time talking to Sergeant Hollis at the reception, didn't she?"

"Yeah, I noticed that too. I think Lennie's smitten."

"Yeah," I thought, "I'd love to see Steph happy and settled, maybe then she'd get the idea out of her head that the Providential Building Society was out to kill her. Such a weird notion anyway."

Jay nudged me gently with his elbow as he offered the bottle and filled our glasses again, the champagne slightly less bubbly now but still fizzing crazily as I gulped it down, saying, "Do you know, Mr. Sutherland, I could get a taste for this?"

"You mean the champagne, Mrs. Sutherland?"

"I mean everything, this place, the sun, the sea, the sand, yeah, and the champagne."

"Hmm, we'd need funds, and there is a way. You could write a book about everything that's happened over the past few months."

"What, you mean, the cold case, the dogs, the bones?"

"Yeah, everything, no holds barred."

"What, and call it something like, um, I don't know, *"A Story of Dogs and Bones?"*

"Yeah, that sounds great, but how about *"A Tale of Dogs and Bones?* As in a dog's tail?"

"Yeah, you're right. I'll have a go then."

"Not yet, though." He took the champagne glass from my hand and set it aside. "After all, we are on our honeymoon." Gently, he pushed me down, so I lay on my back. He leaned over me, and his eyes gazed into mine.

The sun shone warm and heavy, and its tendrils touched my skin and my hair, and my heart beat hard and fast as Jay's lips met mine in a kiss so explosive, if I'd been wearing socks, I'm pretty sure it would have blown them off.

"When I'm down beside the sea, I'm beside myself with glee, Beside the seaside! Beside the sea!

The End

Debbie Chase (married name Debbie Spink) was born in Emsworth in Hampshire in 1959 but has lived in West Yorkshire since 1979. She is the eldest of five children (two sisters and two brothers) and has many nieces and nephews, great-nieces and nephews, aunties, uncles and cousins, having come from a very large family. She has been married since 1984 and has one daughter, Lara, and three cats Ruby, Teddy and Maurice.

She has always been a reader and has enjoyed writing since school. Her proudest moment being when she achieved an A+ for an essay! She has had many short stories and poems for adults and children published in books and magazines. She has written five self-published books, the first being part fact/part fiction and called "You to Me Are Everything." The second book based on a real-life pet-sitting job is called "The Confessions of a Pet Sitter (from the Pet's Point of View), and the third, the sequel to that book, "What a Catastrophe (Teddy's Tale). The fourth book is a book of poems, "I Wasn't There," and the fifth is a murder mystery, "Whatever Happened to George England."

She has also had nine pocket novels published with "My Weekly" magazine, "Planning on Love," "Romance on the Run," "Puppy Love,", "Esther Baby," "Double Trouble" also known as "The Doppelganger," "The Crying Game," "Rachel's War," "Birdie" and "Number One Fan." Her other novels, "Educating Maggie" "A Step Back in Time," "Ruby Tuesday," "The Haunting of Pear Tree Cottage," "The Gift," and the "Mannequin Mystery," are published here with World Castle Publishing, with another novel "My Sweet Valentine," coming soon. All her novels are available to buy online.

Her hobbies are weight training, walking, running, yoga, kettlebell workouts and Pilates. After many years of office work, pub work, and shop work, she is now partially retired and, as well as writing books, works part-time as a Dog Walker/Pet Sitter (Woof Woof Walkies) with her daughter, and as an Examination Invigilator in a local school, and is also a House Experience Volunteer at East Riddlesden Hall, an old manor house open to the public, in Keighley.

Visit her website at: https://www.debbiechase.rocks/